BLOOD ON THE ICE

This was no murder-suicide. In fact, on the face of it, these two deaths were not suspicious at all. Taken together, they would not even add up to a simple mystery. The bodies of Stacy Lapkin and Sergei Bodachenko had been found two miles from the research station, in a dozen bloody pieces, spread over three hundred square feet of ice. The initial conclusion was that these two unfortunates had been attacked and partially eaten by polar bears.

Every person at Immaluost, Russian or American, military or civilian, knew that a polar bear attack was always a possibility at I'm Lost Station.

It was just one of many occupational hazards of the place.

JAG

Clean Steel

ROBERT TINE

*Based on the hit CBS-TV series
created by Donald P. Bellisario*

BERKLEY BOULEVARD BOOKS, NEW YORK

This is a work of fiction. Names, characters, places, and incidents are
either the product of the author's imagination or are used fictitiously,
and any resemblance to actual persons, living or dead, business
establishments, events, or locales is entirely coincidental.

JAG: CLEAN STEEL

A Berkley Boulevard Book / published by arrangement with
Paramount Pictures Corporation

PRINTING HISTORY
Berkley Boulevard edition / April 2000

The Penguin Putnam Inc. World Wide Web site address is
http://www.penguinputnam.com

ISBN: 0-425-16854-9

BERKLEY BOULEVARD
Berkley Boulevard Books are published by The Berkley Publishing Group,
a division of Penguin Putnam Inc., 375 Hudson Street,
New York, New York 10014.
BERKLEY BOULEVARD and its logo
are trademarks belonging to Penguin Putnam Inc.

PRINTED IN THE UNITED STATES OF AMERICA

10 9 8 7 6 5 4 3 2 1

editor's note ✈

This novel is set during season four of *JAG*.

one

AMONG THE MEMBERS OF THE AMERICAN MIL-
itary it is a widely held opinion that, without a doubt,
one of the worst places for assignment in the entire U.S.
armed forces is a cold, barren place so far away from
the equator you don't have to travel too much farther
north to find yourself heading south again.

That place is the United States Air Force base in
Thule, Greenland.

But contrary to this popular belief, Thule is *not* the
worst place you can be sent as a soldier. As it happens,
it is only a runner-up.

A far worse place is actually four hundred miles
northeast of Thule, a little-known, godforsaken military
post that would not exist unless warfare and science had
conspired to create it.

It is an island, a snow-covered speck of ancient lava,
surrounded by ice and located in the Greenland Sea,
barely noticeable on a map. It's name is Immaluost.

And it is not a nice place.

The United States Navy Immaluost Research Station
is one of the worst duty stations in the world as far as
military assignments go. The facility is a small one, so
it has not been the graveyard for too many careers. But

those unlucky enough to be stationed there over the years have usually hated it with a cold intensity.

Immaluost Station—or "I'm Lost" as it is also called—is a collection of prefabricated buildings: a half-dozen labs, where the actual research goes on; two buildings that serve as barracks; an administration block; some outbuildings housing generating and heating equipment; and a mess hall, all connected by a series of long, tubular passageways. Overall, it is a drab, cramped, uncomfortable little place, stuck amidst thousands of square miles of heavy snow, thick ice, and the very cold sea. With the exception of the ice-core scientists for whom Immaluost has been a research paradise, no one in their right mind would want to be there.

The most notable feature of the installation was a 240-foot icebreaker vessel, the USCGC *Polar Star*. Tied up to the aging concrete pier close by the research facility, the *Polar Star* was the primary mainstay of Immaluost, a refuge of last resort should some disaster occur at the research station.

The *Polar Star* was an antique vessel, however. While in good shape and seaworthy, it was approaching forty years of age. Its most modern innovation was the HH-65A Dolphin carried on a small helipad near the stern. The HH-65A was not an evacuation vehicle, however. It could carry only a few people onboard and its tanks held just about enough fuel to make it down to Thule in good weather. If a storm blew it off course, or if the helo was flying over weight, it would never make its destination.

Apart from the cold and discomfort of Immaluost, there was another factor that made assignment there a very unpleasant situation. The research facility was actually a joint venture of the U.S. Navy and the Russian Federated Republic. This partnership, signed by both countries back in the early 1990s, might have looked good on paper. But although the Cold War was over, putting together two sets of military men who had spent most of their adult life training to kill the other did not make for a totally problem-free situation.

Then there were the women.

There were three of them—among sixty-one men. Two of the women—both Russian—were middle-aged, married, and members of the ice-core scientific team. They were constituted members of the station's aristocracy. The third woman was a U.S. Navy nurse, Lieutenant (junior grade) Stacy Lapkin. She'd had the misfortune of receiving Immaluost as her first assignment after completing Officer Indoctrination School in Newport, Rhode Island, a couple of months earlier.

Stacy was a pretty, young woman. Blond hair, big blue eyes, a look of perpetual amazement on her face—she was very much the girl next door. As the only ''eligible'' female in the unit, Stacy attracted a great deal of attention from the men posted to I'm Lost. For the most part, this was good-natured and unthreatening. But there were a few men in the unit—both Russian and American—who were a bit more forward than they should have been. And this had made Stacy's life more than a little difficult. However, she was loath to report any unwanted attentions to the unit commander. Navy women had learned long ago that bringing charges that even hinted of sexual harassment could be a minefield career-wise.

So, Lieutenant Lapkin did her best to grin and bear it, steering away any unwelcome attentions and quietly putting in for a transfer.

Unfortunately for Stacy, that transfer was still three weeks away when she was discovered out on the ice, dead. There was a Russian scientist with her—a man named Sergei Bodachenko. It was thought that he was either her lover or her rapist; there was evidence of sexual activity on Stacy's remains. But no one could ask him.

He was dead, too . . .

This was no murder-suicide. In fact, on the face of it, these two deaths were not suspicious at all. Taken together, they would not even add up to a simple mystery. The bodies of Stacy Lapkin and Sergei Bodachenko had been found two miles from the research station, in a dozen bloody pieces, spread over three hundred square feet of ice. The initial conclusion was that these two unfortunates had been attacked and partially eaten by polar bears.

Every person at Immaluost, Russian or American, military or civilian, knew that a polar bear attack was always a possibility at I'm Lost Station.

It was just one of many occupational hazards of the place.

two ✈

LIEUTENANT COMMANDER JONATHAN THORPE
sat slumped behind the desk in his tiny office inside the
prefabricated administration building of the Immaluost
Research Station.

Outside the wind was howling fiercely. He closed his
eyes and rubbed his temples and cursed the sound; that,
and the constant, ever-present hum of generators spinning in the powerhouse next door.

He was a thin, wiry man, pale-faced with a buzz cut
showing signs of graying at the temples. His hands always seemed to be in motion, an unconscious effort to
keep them warm. His face rarely displayed anything but
a frown.

He said aloud, "This is not the way things were supposed to turn out . . . not at all."

Somewhere along the line—Thorpe was not even sure
where or when—his naval career had fallen off the rails.
He had graduated from the United States Naval Academy at Annapolis. And while not a distinguished stu-
dent—he had placed somewhere in the middle of his
class—an academy diploma was supposed to count for
something in the service, wasn't it?

Besides that, he had served aboard three major vessels, had done a tour at the Naval War College, and had busted his chops with a long stint in the Office of Personnel Administration in the Pentagon.

There was nothing in his personnel folder that suggested that he was in any way suited to run Ice Station I'm Lost. And there was certainly nothing in his past that suggested he should be running a mysterious death investigation either.

Yet now here he was, doing both.

He opened his eyes and looked at the man sitting across the desk from him.

"You understand what I'm saying, Jake? I just wasn't cut out for this assignment," Thorpe moaned. "I'm not like you. You were meant to be way the hell up here, in the ice and snow. This is your turf. You've never sailed warm-water duty in your life, have you?"

"Once. Hated it."

Commander Albert "Jake" McKinney, U.S. Coast Guard, looked like a sailor. Tall and muscular, he had a rugged, weather-beaten face that suggested he'd spent years in the wind and rain, guiding his ship through the blackest of nights and the roughest of waters. Wrinkles around his dark eyes told of long hours of looking out the horizon, forehead creased against the sun shimmering on deep water or blue ice. There was no doubt that the bridge of a ship was his natural habitat.

At forty-three, he was five years older than Thorpe, and holding the rank of commander, captain of the icebreaker *Polar Star*, he was technically Thorpe's superior. But McKinney wanted no part of Thorpe's frozen nightmare. He was quite happy running his ship and providing support for the miserable men under Thorpe's command.

He smiled sympathetically at his friend. "Have you contacted Thule about the deaths yet?"

Up there, the military chain of command ran ʋ̶
from Immaluost through the air base at Thule and then
out to the world beyond. Sometimes it seemed like it
was a million miles long.

"Yes," Thorpe replied, sighing heavily. "I did. . . ."

"And?" McKinney asked. "What kind of instructions did they give you?"

"Absolutely none," Thorpe replied. "The air force isn't going to touch this. They have a perfectly good CID unit based down there, but they claim they aren't allowed to do cross-service investigations, especially ones involving fatalities."

"Well, that makes sense, I guess," McKinney said. "Besides, what the hell do you want the air force investigating a naval matter for?"

Thorpe shrugged. "I really don't give a damn who looks into it," he replied. "If Sherlock Holmes and a bunch of Scotland Yard bobbies showed up here and took this out of my lap, I wouldn't make a peep."

"Well, I don't think Sherlock's coming," said McKinney with a laugh. "Do you?"

"Unfortunately not."

There was a knock on the office door. Thorpe slumped deeper into his chair.

"Oh, God," he said unhappily. "That'll be the Russians."

Though their communist state was dead, there still seemed to be in every Russian a lasting imprint, namely, a general acceptance that officialdom had a role to play in every event, both public and private.

It was no surprise to the leader of the Russian team, Dr. Oleg Oblomov, that there was to be an investigation into the deaths of the scientist and the nurse.

7

His first question to Thorpe after coming through the door, however, was why this investigation was going to be conducted by an American military unit and not a Russian one.

Oblomov stated his argument simply.

"This is a joint operation, Commander Thorpe," he said. "Therefore there must be a joint investigation."

"That is not necessarily true, Doctor," Thorpe replied. "This station is operated under the aegis of the United States Navy and it is the United States Navy that is responsible for investigations of this kind."

Oblomov bit his lip. While he was aware that he had certain protocols he could insist upon, it was also plain that the U.S. Navy had the upper hand in the control of Ice Station Immaluost. Oblomov was always fighting a rear-guard action against further American domination, and it was usually a losing battle. But now, with the death of one of his men, he knew his superiors at the Russian Institute of Meteorological and Atmospheric Studies would not want to him to cede one more inch of authority to the Americans. That's really what he was here to argue about.

But before he spoke again, he glanced at McKinney, who was still in the office.

"Perhaps it would be best if we continued this discussion just between us, Lieutenant Commander Thorpe," Oblomov said. Like most Russians, he had a built-in suspicion of westerners.

"Commander McKinney is the senior officer here," Thorpe replied. "Anything you say to me can be heard by him."

Oblomov took a deep breath.

"All right, then," he began. "It is my duty to insist that some sort of Russian presence be allowed in this investigation. It is in keeping with the jointity of this operation.''

Thorpe wondered if he should point out that there was no such word as ''jointity,'' but decided that it would not be a proper diplomatic move at this juncture. On the whole, Thorpe knew Oblomov was under certain political pressures that did not apply to members of the American half of the team. In this regard, Thorpe actually felt a little sorry for the Russian.

''Really, Doctor, there is no need for two teams to investigate a single incident. I mean, I assume you're not suggesting that a Russian team investigate the death of Sergei and an American team investigate the death of Lieutenant Lapkin?''

Oblomov shook his head. ''No, of course not. That would be far from the spirit of jointity.''

Thorpe raised his hands, palms up. ''Then what *are* you suggesting, Doctor?''

''That I be allowed to report this incident immediately,'' he replied. ''And if the institute insists, an investigation team must be allowed to come here to observe—at the very least.''

Thorpe sighed. ''I cannot promise any Russian investigative team will be permitted to work at Ice Station Immaluost. But you are welcome to report these sad events to your superiors—and let them take whatever measures they deem necessary.''

''Thank you, Lieutenant Commander.''

''Don't mention it,'' Thorpe replied. ''Anything for the spirit of 'jointity.' ''

The Russian left with a slight bow, and McKinney and Thorpe were alone again.

McKinney poured them both a cup of coffee.

''I hope you didn't open a very big can of worms just

now," McKinney said, handing Thorpe a steaming cup. "I mean, why is there any need for an investigation in the first place?"

"What do you mean?" Thorpe asked, sipping his coffee.

McKinney just shrugged. "What's to investigate? Sergei and Lieutenant Lapkin ignored safety regulations, went out on the far ice, and were attacked by polar bears. . . . The picture seems pretty clear to me."

Thorpe put his cup down and rubbed his temples again.

"Think about it for a minute, though," he began. "You knew Sergei, right?"

McKinney nodded.

"Smart guy, for a Russian, don't you agree?"

Again McKinney nodded. "I'd almost say he was brilliant—if one can be brilliant and still want to study ice."

"Exactly," Thorpe said. "So, in your experience, was Sergei really the type not to use his flare gun or pistol? From the first days of this experiment we have warned everyone about the polar bears up here. There are notices all over the place."

"What are you saying, exactly?" McKinney asked, stumped.

"What I'm saying—and it is still very confidential at this point—is that both Sergei and Lieutenant Lapkin were carrying their weapons when they were killed, yet there is no evidence that they used them. No found shell casings at the site. Nothing."

McKinney sat back, looked at the ceiling, pondering this.

"Well, where are the weapons *now*? Perhaps we can determine if they've been fired or not," he finally offered.

Thorpe went back to rubbing his temples. "That's the strange part," he said, eyes closed. "We can't find the weapons."

McKinney just stared back at him.

"Can't find them? Whatever do you mean?"

"I mean, they were not recovered," Thorpe told him. "They were not picked up with the bodies. At first everyone thought those two fools went out onto the ice without them. But we counted the stockpile and two pistols and two flare guns are missing. Signed out to them."

McKinney just shook his head. "There's got to be a mistake. What are you saying? That the polar bears carried off their weapons? Or they ate them, too?"

Thorpe just stared back at him. "Does that make sense to you?"

McKinney thought about it for a moment.

"No, I guess not," he said finally.

"Which is precisely why there will be an investigation," said Thorpe evenly. "To answer questions just like that."

He rubbed his temples once again. He'd been to Fiji once—it was a port visit on his first sea tour years ago. Whenever he rubbed his temples very hard, a vision of Fiji's flowing palms and crystal water popped into his head.

"That's why I've got to keep two bodies on ice for God knows how long," he went on, opening his eyes and coming back to reality. "Plus, I've got a research station that is probably so rampant with rumors by now, it's going to drive itself collectively nuts."

McKinney just grunted. "You can't help that, Johnny. That's just how things are in places like this."

"I know," said Thorpe, "but you forget one other thing, Jake. Something very important."

"Yeah? What's that?"

"Someone in this place might be a murderer," said Thorpe grimly. "And until we prove otherwise, how is anyone supposed to sleep easy knowing that?"

"Murder?" McKinney nearly spit the word out. "You're not seriously thinking that—"

"I've *got to* consider everything," Thorpe interrupted him. "Including foul play. There's a hole in every possible explanation of these events. And by God, if I screw this thing up, there really is nowhere else the navy can send me."

McKinney sipped his coffee. Thorpe was making sense.

"But who is going to investigate this from our end?" he finally asked. "I mean, you just gave Ivan there the okay to report what happened. He could have half the Russian military up here inside of a week. Who on our end is going to keep that type of thing under control?"

Thorpe thought for a long moment, and then suddenly a smile spread wide across his face—a very rare occurrence. He might have been assigned to the worst post in the U.S. Navy—and indeed in the whole of the U.S. armed forces. But that didn't mean he didn't have friends in higher places.

"I'm not sure, exactly," he said. "But I'll wager there's a team of JAG lawyers somewhere that's about to get a very nasty surprise. . . ."

three ✈

IT WAS RAINING.

Not the gentle autumn rain usually associated with an early October day. No, this was a hard rain. Cold, blustery.

Ominous. . . .

The C-141 cargo jet was waiting on the tarmac at Edwards Air Force Base, engines turning, ready to go. It was already twenty minutes late for takeoff. The air force crew was getting very impatient. This was not going to be a pleasant flight for them. It was going to prove long and arduous, and the weather was practically guaranteed not to be cooperative.

What's more, the huge jet had been mustered to carry just three passengers. Navy personnel. And one of them was late.

Finally a navy staff car roared up to the runway and headed for the waiting jet. It stopped fifty feet away from the open tail door and the stocky figure of Bud Roberts climbed out. Lieutenant (junior grade) Bud Roberts quickly retrieved his two travel bags from the car's

13

trunk, thanked the driver, and ran as fast as he could to the waiting jet.

He threw his bags inside and felt a hand grab his own and haul him into the airplane. He landed, unceremoniously, flat on his face. No sooner was he aboard when the airplane began taxiing.

Bud rolled over and found himself staring up at two smiling faces. One was Major Sarah Mackenzie. The other was Lieutenant Commander Harmon Rabb, Jr.

"Am I glad to see you sir . . . and ma'am," Bud said, scrambling to his feet.

"Likewise, Lieutenant," Harm said. "You're carrying our orders, I presume?"

Bud started patting himself down, reaching inside of every pocket before finally finding a long, yellow envelope.

He handed the packet to Harm just as the big airplane reached the end of the runway. "These are our orders," he said.

The huge airplane began vibrating mightily. Its engines were running up to full scream.

"We'd better get strapped in," Mac suggested.

The interior of the Starlifter was vast, empty, and cold. There was a small section of jump seats about halfway up the fuselage. They made their way to these seats and were strapped in by the time the huge aircraft took to the air. Once airborne, it immediately turned north.

Mac shivered. "I hope they can pump some heat to us back here," she said. "I have a feeling this is going to be a long flight."

Both Harm and Mac were wearing heavy woolen travel clothes. Bud, however, had a long, civilian raincoat on, with very civilian attire underneath. He had been on his way for a week of leave—a second honeymoon of sorts—when he'd received the call from Admiral A. J. Chegwidden. Leave canceled. Pick up orders from JAG headquarters and meet Harm and Mac at Andrews.

To say Bud was not dressed for the occasion was a vast understatement. He pulled his raincoat tighter to his body and felt the same chill Mac did.

"Does that clear up the mystery?" he asked Harm as he read over the first of two documents contained in the packet.

"Clears up one and opens several more," Harm said, passing the first document to Mac.

"We have a case of two unexplained deaths at a very remote scientific station up in the arctic, a place called Immaluost Island," he began. "At the moment foul play is not suspected . . . but it has not been ruled out. The admiral wants us to look into it, make sure everything is shipshape during the upcoming investigation. Wants us to run it, in fact."

Mac shivered again. "I'm glad I brought my flannel pajamas," she said.

Harm smiled and gave her a wink. "Me too," he said.

But now Bud began squirming in his seat. "May I ask a question, sir?" he finally piped up.

"Sure, Lieutenant. . . ."

"Why us, sir? We're JAGs. Isn't this like sending lawyers to do detectives' work?"

Harm smiled broadly. "Bud, let me recite the rules in the world of JAG," he said. "Rule number one: Ours is not to wonder why, ours is to do what the admiral tells us to do."

Bud tightened his raincoat around him again.

"Rule number two," Harm went on, "I suspect that in the admiral's infinite wisdom he may foresee a situation in which one of the navy personnel at this research facility might need legal assistance. And the way the weather changes up there—well, it's better to have us on the ground, than trying to get through."

Bud squirmed a bit more in his seat.

"And rule number three," Harm continued, "when the son of an old friend of the admiral's asks for JAG's help, the admiral does not turn him down."

"The commander of this station is the admiral's god-son," Mac explained to Bud, rereading a section of the orders. "His father and the admiral fought in Vietnam together. The father died several years ago, but the son is still close to the boss. That's why we are going north."

Harm smiled again. "Besides, I thought you liked the snow, Lieutenant?"

Bud began stammering. "I . . . I d-do sir," he said. "I mean . . . I do and I don't. It depends. You know, on what the season is."

"Well, where we're going, there's only two seasons a year," Mac said, finishing the document. "Night and day. This place is only a stone's throw from the North Pole itself."

"And it being October," Harm said looking out the small window, "a slow night is beginning to fall. Pretty soon, they won't be seeing any sun up there at all."

They were all silent for a while. The big airplane finally passed out of the rainstorm and climbed into the darker skies above.

"May I ask why these two deaths are so unexplained?" Bud said, finally breaking the silence.

Mac looked on the second page of the orders, under the section about the cause of death, and let out a little groan.

"Oh, gross," she said, passing the page to Harm. "What a way to go. . . ."

Harm read the information—and felt his stomach do a flip.

"Well, that certainly is unpleasant."

"Is there something I should know?" Bud asked them anxiously.

Harm just passed the order sheet to him. He read it and gasped.

"Polar bears?"

He slumped further down into his seat.

"Boy, I think I should have stayed in bed this morning," he groaned.

Harm and Mac just eyed each other.

"And miss all the fun?" Harm asked.

Four ✈

IT HAD BEEN A VERY BAD MOON CYCLE FOR the Ininitka family.

Things just weren't going right. The Ininitkas were a fishing community located on the northeast tip of Immaluost Island. Their settlement had existed for more than four hundred years. At present, more than 150 people lived there, all members of the rather extended Ininitka family.

They fished for herring and salmon, using both spears and nets. They owned two engine-powered squalls, made of wood and metal and driven by diesel engines. They also had many smaller canoes and kayaks, most of them painted bright red and yellow and festooned with drawings of birds and whales and images of the northern lights—these were thought to bring them good luck while fishing.

But things were going badly these days. The fish were not jumping into the nets as they had for centuries. Their two powered fishing boats had both sprung leaks in the past week; one had almost sunk. Many of their canoes and kayaks were springing leaks, too.

The seals were not cooperating, either. The very extended Ininitka family relied on catching at least ten seals per week: their meat and oil and hides and bones were essential to the family's well-being. They would be extremely important in sustaining the Ininitkas through the cold dark nights ahead. Winter was coming, and up here, near the top of the world, it would last six long months.

All of this was weighing heavily on the shoulders of the family's shaman, an ancient man named Mook. After much study and prayer and meditation, Mook had sadly declared the last moon cycle as one of the ten worst in the Ininitkas' long history. And while pronouncing this finding at a family gathering a few days before, Mook had been forced to admit that he did not yet know why this bad cycle had suddenly descended on his people. He'd studied the family's oral traditions for days before making the declaration, trying to spot a clue, a reason for the recent misfortunes. But he'd found none.

That's why Mook was now sitting in his hut, his oil lamp flickering away, reading over the family's fishing logs. Unlike his traditional stories which he kept in his head, the fishing logs were written history, meticulous entries made every week for years, to track the settlement's fortunes in hunting at sea.

He'd been reading these by firelight for many, many hours, and now his eyes were tired. He got up, sipped some black water from his cup, and took a moment to breathe. He could stop now, and read the rest of the fishing histories tomorrow. Or he could press on into the sleeping time, and finish the dour task. He closed his eyes and held his hand to his chest and tried to conjure up the face of his grandfather, old Meekita. What should I do? he asked this spirit.

"Continue on," was the spirit's reply.

So Mook eased himself back down into his seal-fur chair and picked up the old log book again and started reading. And within a minute's time, he'd found his clue.

The family *had* gone through a bad time similar to this.

It had occurred almost fifty years before.

When Mook realized this, he felt a cold chill go through him, not a natural feeling for an Ininitka.

Sitting in his hut, the fire in his lamp fading fast, fifty years flashed back in the blink of his old, tired eyes. He'd been a young boy back then, not even a teenager. Such things as bad fishing times were kept from him by the elders.

But he remembered them now.

"The white hairs," he whispered. "They are the ones who caused this. . . ."

No sooner were the words out of his mouth when an urgent banging came to his hut's door.

Mook got up to answer the knocking. But before he could raise himself from his seat, the door flew open and one of his young nephews burst in.

His name was Week-wa.

"Uncle . . . ," he gasped, trying to catch his breath, "big trouble."

Mook stared into his nephew's eyes and did not like what he saw.

He took the boy by the shoulders and sat him down. He went to close the door and saw that there were at least a dozen other people outside his hut, staring in. They all looked very frightened.

Mook closed the door on them and then returned to his nephew. Week-wa was sitting nervously, looking up at Mook and waiting for the signal to speak.

Mook poured him a cup of black water, gave it to

him, and waited for Week-wa to drink it. Only then did the teenager catch his breath and settle down a bit.

Mook pulled his chair up closer to him, added some oil to the ceremonial lamp, and placed his hands on Week-wa's knees.

"Now, tell me," he began. "What trouble have you encountered?"

Week-wa just looked back at him.

"I saw them, Great Uncle," Week-wa said, his voice trembling. "I never really believed in them. I'm sorry I have to say that. But now . . . now, I do believe. Because . . ."

He gulped more black water.

"Because . . . I saw them. . . ."

Mook gripped his nephew's knees. His intuition told him that the news he was about to receive was not going to be good at all. Still, he had to know.

"Saw what, nephew? What has frightened you so?"

Week-wa looked up at him again, tears filling the corners of his eyes.

"The lights . . . under the ice . . ." he began. "I saw them. Just now . . . out in No Seals Bay."

Mook took his hands from his nephew's knees. His breath caught in his throat.

"This is blasphemy if it's not the truth you speak," Mook said, his own voice trembling now. "If this is a lie, I have the authority to put you out on the ice and banish you forever. . . ."

Week-wa drained the cup of black water.

"Don't you think I know that, Great Uncle?" he said. "Do you think I would come here, like this, if I was making it up?"

Mook stared into Week-wa's eyes and knew his nephew was not lying. He reached over and held his head in his hands and comforted the boy. But his own heart suddenly felt like it had fallen to his feet.

The lights under the ice. . . .

These were words he thought he would never hear. But now, along with the bad luck the family had encountered, they sounded ominous—and not totally unexpected.

"What shall I do, Great Uncle?" Week-wa asked him desperately. "Will my eyeballs fall out, like the legends say?"

Mook patted his cheek reassuringly. "If such a disaster was going to happen, it would have happened by now," he told his nephew.

Then he stood him up and gave him a hug.

"Tell no one else what you have seen," he whispered in Week-wa's ear. "And those you have told, give them no more information. Stay in your hut, stay warm, and think of your grandfather, and the good things he did for the family so long ago. If you do all this, you will be all right."

Week-wa's demeanor eased considerably. Apparently his eyeballs were not going to fall out.

But what did his vision mean for the family as a whole?

"Do not worry about that," Mook told him, answering his question before he could ask it. "That's what I am here for."

He took a long, deep breath, but the chill would not go away.

"I will take care of it," Mook said finally. "Just like my grandfather did when the white hairs came here the first time. . . ."

Five ✈

"I'M LOST" STATION WAS SO ISOLATED, A visit by anyone from the outside world usually turned into a big occasion.

The visitor was most likely flown in from Thule, 376 miles to the south. The means of transport was almost always a huge CH-53 Sea Stallion helicopter, specially outfitted for the harsh polar environment. Once word went through the station that a flight was incoming, a welcoming committee of sorts would be organized. The official greeters would don the silliest costumes they could come up with and frequently meet the arriving chopper with a barrage of snowballs.

Any visitors from Thule would usually stay over for a forty-eight-hour period—the flights were less frequent on the winter nights. They would be honored at a dinner attended by all and usually peppered with questions about how life was progressing Down There, in Thule, as if that were the center of the universe, which to the people at I'm Lost, it was.

But there was no greeting committee for the helicopter now slowly circling the big orange-and-black helipad located on the southern end of the Immaluost facility.

Things had not been the same since the deaths of

Lieutenant Lapkin and Sergei Bodachenko. The gruesome aspect of their demise, still thought of as a meal for polar bears, had sent a collective chill throughout the place that no amount of diesel-powered heat could sufficiently erase. Thorpe had conducted a refresher course on polar bear safety two days after the bodies had been discovered, but this did little to allay the fears of those at the station, either.

Just as the navy commander had predicted, rumors were running rampant around the facility. By one story, the two unfortunates, star-crossed lovers by now, had had a terrible row. Stacy had fled out to the tundra. Sergei followed, and when he saw her attacked by the bears, he tried in vain to save her and was thus killed, too.

Another scenario had Sergei following Stacy out to the high outcrop of rock where the bodies were found, somehow raping her there, then murdering her, only to have a pack of bears show up and devour them both, he while still alive, she, mercifully, already dead.

But there was now an even darker rumor making the rounds; some said it originated from the Russian camp, others said it was a wholly American-cooked piece of gossip. This story had no definable actions, no bawdy-cum-grisly blood sites. This one simply asked a question, one that Thorpe had hoped to keep confidential. If the two had gone out onto the ice, they had to have brought their flare guns and pistols with them. A count of the weapons at the facility had proven that they'd done just that. Yet where were these weapons now? They had not been found with the bodies—everyone was sure of that much.

So, did the polar bears carry them away? Why were there no spent casings found around the bodies? If the two were armed, would they not have fought off the bears with their weapons? And even if they had been taken by surprise by the creatures, where were their weapons now?

There were no answers to these questions—not yet, anyway.

Now, as the big CH-53 helicopter began descending, the only person waiting for it was Lieutenant Commander Thorpe.

The helo came in with a bounce, kicking up a blizzard of snow with its huge rotors. Its pilots killed the engines as quickly as possible, and the storm of ice and snow settled down.

The side door opened and two people tumbled out. They quickly helped out a third. The three figures duck-walked toward Thorpe who was motioning them his way.

"Lieutenant Commander Harm Rabb," Harm said with a brisk salute.

Thorpe returned it and shook Harm's hand.

"Major Sarah Mackenzie and Lieutenant JG Bud Roberts," Harm said, introducing his partners.

Thorpe shook hands with both and then said, "Glad to have you all here—though I sure wish it were under better circumstances."

"As do we," Harm agreed.

Thorpe pointed toward the facility's mess hall. "Let's get warm and get some coffee into you," he suggested.

They reached the mess hall's outer heat room in short order and began climbing out of the heavy parkas that had been given to them on their arrival at Thule air base.

All three were tired—the flight from Andrews to Thule had been a long, bumpy frigid affair. Landing at Thule had been a skidding, tousling situation. The only good thing about the ice-covered air base was they didn't have to stay there too long. A helo had already been waiting for them when they'd arrived. Issuing the heavy clothes had taken but a few minutes. They were quickly put on the big chopper for the long ride north to Immaluost Station.

Their whirlwind time on the ground at Thule left them with the definite impression that the air force wanted to get rid of them as quickly as possible, which is just what they'd done.

Inside the heat room now their skin began to drip with water—just a few moments out in the frigid air had caused the condensation to stick to their faces. It was now rolling off them like tears.

Both Harm and Mac were still wearing their working uniforms under the parkas—heavy overalls not unlike those that pilots wore during flight ops. But Bud had been notified of this mission at the last moment and thus had not had the luxury of climbing into the proper arctic wear. He'd kept his raincoat wrapped tightly around him during the entire trip up to Thule and then to I'm Lost.

Now seeing his predicament, Thorpe innocently handed him a pair of arctic overalls similar to those Harm and Mac were wearing. Bud hesitated, however.

"Problems, Bud?" Harm asked, noting his reluctance to take the overalls.

"Well, sir," Bud began stammering. "I'm just a bit, well, shy about this clothes-changing stuff. . . ."

Mac laughed. "I'll turn my head, Bud," she said. "If that's what you're worried about. . . ."

Bud's face turned beet-red.

"No, ma'am," he said. "That's not necessary. I mean, it is. I mean . . . I don't want you to look. I mean . . ."

Harm reached over and clamped his hand atop Bud's mouth. This served to stop Bud in mid-sentence.

"Just tell us, Bud," Harm said. "What is the problem?"

Bud's face turned even redder, if that was possible.

He slowly began unbuttoning his rain coat. Beneath he was wearing what was probably the loudest, gaudiest, Hawaiian-style flower shirt ever created.

"Whoa!" Harm cried. "That thing is bright enough to land Tomcats at night."

"Did I bring my sunglasses?" Mac asked facetiously. "I'm going to need them."

Bud took the ribbing like a man, but it was clear he was greatly embarrassed.

"You must remember something," he said in his defense. "I was ready to go on vacation leave when I got Petty Officer Tiner's call. I didn't have the time to climb into my foul weather gear."

Harm and Mac just couldn't stop laughing. But then Thorpe stepped in and put his arm around Bud's shoulder.

"Don't you worry, Lieutenant," he said. "You're about to find out that you are actually quite in fashion here."

Bud was confused. They all were.

"What do you mean, sir?" he asked.

Thorpe smiled and removed his outer jacket. He, too, was wearing a very loud Hawaiian-type shirt. If anything it was even brighter than Bud's.

"We all wear them off duty," the station commander explained. "It's a sort of in-joke."

Harm and Mac just stared at the two men, standing amidst a pile of snow and boots, wearing shirts that would make Don Ho blush.

"You see?" Thorpe said to all of them, a bit of seriousness creeping into his voice. "Not many things up here are what they seem."

• • •

They moved into the mess hall from the heat room through a short tunnel.

Many of the buildings in the research facility were connected this way. The tunnels—about seven feet around and held in place by air pressure alone, allowed the station personnel to transit from building to building without necessitating going outside.

The mess hall was remarkably well-appointed considering the fact that they were very close to the top of the world. It looked like a very ritzy cafeteria. There were long, spacious tables with many comfortably padded chairs orbiting them. There were two buffet-style tables set up—both had many trays of steaming food waiting for whoever might pass by.

Harm glanced at the offerings and saw freshly cooked roast beef, turkey, ham, steaming soups, pasta, and fresh greens. Many beverages were also on display—soda, coffee, and three kinds of milk: whole, low-fat, and chocolate.

"Watch this," Harm whispered to Mac.

Sure enough, Bud made a beeline for the case containing the chocolate milk.

"You can take the boy out of the city, but . . ." Mac said, ending in a shared laugh with Harm.

They took a cup of coffee and joined Thorpe at an isolated table. Sure enough, many of the people currently inside the mess hall were wearing Hawaiian shirts. Indeed, Mac and Harm looked rather out of place.

They spent a few minutes talking about Admiral Chegwidden.

"I've only met him once," Thorpe confessed. "But I know he and my dad were real tight. When this whole mess came up, and I knew that I had to play my cards right, he was really the only person I thought I could turn to."

"You made the right choice," Harm told him. "The admiral is good to have in your corner when things get dicey. Believe us, we know."

Mac and Bud nodded in full agreement.

Thorpe let out a long sigh. "That's good to hear. And just the fact that he got you three up here so quick— well, I don't know how I'll be able to thank him."

Mac reached over and touched Thorpe's arm reassuringly. "I think the fact that your father and the admiral were such good friend is thanks enough."

Thorpe smiled—again, a very rare occasion.

"Then maybe when this mess is cleared up, I'll ask him to find out why I was sent way up here in the first place. . . ."

Thorpe let his voice trail off.

"Well, like you said," Mac replied, "some things might not be what they seem."

Bud joined them at the table with a massive plate of food and three plastic containers of chocolate milk.

Harm took one look at the plate and rolled his eyes.

"Did you leave any food for the rest of the people, Lieutenant?"

Again Bud was instantly embarrassed. "Oh, sorry, sir," he began. "I mean, it *was* a long trip and I really hadn't eaten anything since . . ."

"Since Thule," Harm filled in for him.

But Thorpe just patted Bud on the back again. "Eat all you want son," he said. "That's one thing we don't have to worry about up here. The food is good and there's plenty of it. . . ."

He paused for a moment.

"Of course, I'm not sure just how much you want to eat before we go in and view the remains," he concluded.

Harm eyed Mac who looked over at Bud who was

just about to devour a huge bite of rare, gravy-soaked roast beef.

"I've seen bodies before," Bud said to Thorpe valiantly. "Part of my job sometimes. I can take it. . . ."

Thorpe sipped his coffee.

"I'm sure you can," he replied. "But I must emphasize something here. I said 'remains,' not bodies."

That was enough to make Bud drop his fork.

Now the tone of the conversation changed. It suddenly got very serious.

"That might be something we should get out of the way as soon as possible," Harm told Thorpe.

"I agree," the commander said. "Are you ready now?"

Harm took one more sip of coffee. "I am," he stated.

Mac nodded, though a bit uncertainly. "It has to be done," she said.

Bud looked at his big plate of food, then pushed it away from him.

"I guess . . . ," he said forlornly.

Retrieving their outerwear, they walked out of the mess hall, past a series of labs, to a building that was located at the very far end of a network of tubes.

It had a big steel door on it with a sign that read AUXILIARY MATERIALS LAB—COLD STORAGE ONLY.

"It was the only place I could think of for storing the remains," Thorpe said, unlocking the door and swinging it open.

A great gust of condensation poured out onto them.

Mac shivered.

"A cold place in a cold place," she said.

"Exactly," Thorpe replied.

They went in, bundling up in their parkas once more.

There were two tables in the middle of the supply room. Each one had a vague, indistinguishable shape on it. Neither looked like a body.

Thorpe walked over to the first table. It had a tag taped to it reading "Sergei B."

"Are you ready?"

Both Harm and Mac steeled themselves; Bud hung back but did not make a sound.

"Yes," Harm said.

Thorpe pulled the cover back.

Harm tried to stay focused but it was a hard thing to do. Thorpe had been right. This was not a body. Rather, it was pieces of one. But it was strange: the pieces were so random and indistinguishable, they didn't look so horrific.

Mac felt the same way. But still, it was obvious that this was a person that had met a terrible end.

"Seen enough?" Thorpe asked them after about ten seconds.

"Not that there is much to see," Harm said.

Thorpe covered the remains.

"Any need to see Lieutenant Lapkin?" he asked.

All three of them shook their heads no.

"That will be okay," Harm said, speaking for all of them. "We get the idea."

They retreated back out into the tunnel.

It was only once they were out of the room that the full impact of what they'd just seen started to sink in. Bud was pale. Mac was being strong. So was Harm.

"What now?" Thorpe asked, locking the storage-room door.

"This might seem like a strange question," Harm began, "but what do you know about polar bears in general?"

Thorpe shrugged. "Only that they are ferocious," he

began. "That we have permission to shoot them on sight. That they are always hungry, and—"

Harm stopped him right there.

"Always hungry?" he cut in. "I imagine they would be, up here. Food being scarce."

"That's why I gather that . . . ," Thorpe confirmed.

"Then why," Harm asked, "are there any remains at all?"

Thorpe seemed puzzled for a moment.

"What do you mean?"

Harm lowered his voice. "Well, looking at this strictly from a polar bear's point of view, I get the feeling that when they find something to eat, they don't let very much of it go to waste."

They were all silent for a moment, letting what Harm had said fully sink in.

Thorpe finally shook his head. "Well, you're right, of course," he said, lowering his voice as well. "And I might add, you're not the first person to think that this might not have involved polar bears at all."

Thorpe quickly told them how Sergei and Lieutenant Lapkin had both checked out pistols and flare guns before leaving the station that day, and that the weapons had still not been recovered.

"Now those guns might still be out in the snow someplace," Thorpe said. "With the weather up here, the landscape can change very quickly and does so frequently. But, until they are accounted for. . . ."

". . . we have to keep all avenues open," Harm said, finishing his sentence for him.

"Right," Thorpe agreed.

Harm thought a moment.

"Okay, now what?" Mac asked.

"I think we have to get those remains down to Thule," Harm said. "I'm sure they can perform a decent autopsy there. At the very least it will give us a good indication of just what we are looking at here.''

"I agree," Thorpe said. "We can send them back with the helo that brought you up here. I can send one of my men along with them.''

Harm thought a moment more, then said, "I agree that they should be accompanied, but I think it should be by someone who was not here during this incident. I hate to be like that, but I think it's wise.''

Thorpe nodded again. "Yes, of course. But who will go with them back to Thule?''

They all turned around and looked directly at Bud.

Bud's face drained of color.

"I thought you said this was going to be fun, Commander!''

six ✈

MOOK'S HANDS WERE SHAKING AS HE ROSE from his bed of fur and began putting on his outer clothes.

This was not going to be a pleasant day for him. Even though he was only fifty-seven years old, he was the oldest person in the family. He did not have the strength of a young man anymore and it had been some time since the last time he'd been out in a kayak alone. But he knew this day he had to do it.

What he had to face, he had to face alone.

In the long tradition of the Ininitka family, the omen of *freeka-doka*—the lights under the ice—was one of the most ominous. They represented very evil spirits operating in what was the most valuable piece of nature to the Ininitkas: the sea. In all his years Mook had never heard of anyone actually seeing *freeka-doka*. His father certainly hadn't. As a young boy, Mook remembered his grandfather mentioning a woman in the family who, nearly one hundred years ago now, had claimed to see the lights under the ice. Her eyeballs had popped out as a result. Or at least that's how the story went.

But now, with his nephew Week-wa's startling report, it was up to Mook, as spiritual leader of the Ininitka, to go to the place where his nephew claimed to have seen *freeka-doka* and see it for himself.

He chose his brother's bright-yellow kayak for this mission. He believed that the drawing of the great blue whale on its skin would bring him good luck; plus, he would be more easily seen by anyone looking for him should he run into trouble.

He left his hut and collected the kayak and brought it down to the beach. The village was still asleep—no one knew he was about to embark on such a dangerous journey. That was the way it had to be. Should he not return, he knew he could count on Week-wa to tell the others what had happened.

They would have to take things from there.

Mook took no black water with him, no sustenance of any kind. This was a journey to find some spirits—very evil spirits. It was well-known that evil spirits could detect the approach of a human being by smell, among other things. To Mook's nose, black water or dried seal meat gave off a very strong odor.

He cast off from the beach and began paddling north. Week-wa had claimed to see the lights under the ice in a region northeast of Immaluost Island known as Maluk-Ta-tuck—No Seals Bay, or more literally, "the place where the seals do not play."

Maluk-Ta-tuck was a strange slice of sea and ice. It was known for freezing over very quickly and at the most unpredictable times, trapping any fishermen who might be caught there. Two of Mook's cousins had died out there ten years before, crushed by the quickly moving ice and then eaten by the crabs—not a pleasant way to meet the ancestors.

So Mook began paddling and singing some prayers and hoping the winds would be with him. Though his bones were old and his muscles not as sharp as they used to be, he found the going easy at first.

The sun was not up yet and when it rose it would not get more than twenty degrees above the horizon. As a young man Mook had loved the coming of the long night. For him, it had meant a time to think and eat and have sex. But now, as an old man, he hated the creeping darkness. He knew he didn't have many years left on earth.

He wished they could all be spent in the sunlight.

It took him an hour to reach Maluk-Ta-tuck. The place was a field of ice sunken to a depth of about ten feet. A small lake of crystal-blue water covered the two-square-miles area, which, in turn, was surrounded by high ice-bergs with only a narrow outlet to the sea.

For the next two hours, Mook paddled and prayed, stopping every few minutes to stare down into the ice. But each time, he saw nothing but his own reflection staring back up at him.

The sun was still not up. A dull red on the horizon was the only natural light. Mook had sang just about every prayer he knew, and still he saw nothing beneath the ice.

This made him feel both happy and sad. He was happy that there was no evidence of lights under the ice—this was at least good news for the family. Because if he had actually seen *freeka-doka*, then great horrors could have descended on them, not to mention the possibility of his own eyeballs falling out.

But he was also sad now as well because he feared his nephew Week-wa was going crazy. There was no other explanation. To claim to have seen *freeka-doka* and not actually have seen them was simply a sign that something had gone wrong with Week-wa's brain and that—

Suddenly the water underneath Mook's kayak started moving. He stared down at it and could no longer see his reflection. The water was rippling so much, it was as if a giant hand had suddenly stuck itself into the lake and was churning it up.

Mook felt his eyes go wide. Then the kayak itself started shaking. *What evil was this?*

That's when Mook turned around and saw something even more horrible than the lights under the ice. It was huge. It was black. It was sharp and pointed and had very strange angles. It had two huge green eyes and two very long, very wide legs that caused it to glide atop the water instead of down upon it.

It was heading right for him!

Mook began paddling furiously, but this thing was moving much too fast to avoid him.

It hit his kayak with a great *crash!* and immediately split it in two.

The last thing Mook heard was the horrible sound of his own scream. . . .

It was Week-wa who found Mook's body late that afternoon.

It had washed up on the Beach of the Sun. His kayak was gone, as was his paddle and his hat.

Week-wa knew that Mook had gone to look for *freeka-doka*. He and the other villagers had been searching for Mook all day. Now, upon seeing his uncle's body on the beach, Week-wa's heart dropped a mile. Two other boys from the village were with him. Gingerly, they approached the frozen, unmoving frame.

Tears were in Week-wa's eyes as they rolled him over and chipped the ice from his face.

"He is dead," one of the other boys said. "We should float him back out to sea."

"Quick!" Week-wa said instead. "We must get him to a warm place."

So they picked him up and ran as fast as they could to the nearest hut, which was the fishing boat repair shop. The men inside saw their plight and helped set Mook's body down next to a fire.

"God, with Mook dead, who will run our lives?" one worker asked. "Who will tell us what to do?"

The other men did not know. They were all close to tears as well.

But then miraculously, Mook's eyes opened.

"Nephew!" he cried.

"Uncle!"

Mook started laughing—he was absolutely astonished to be alive.

"I can see?" he asked them all.

They all laughed with him. "Yes, you can," they all replied.

"Uncle, what happened?" Week-wa asked him urgently. "Did you see the lights under the ice?"

Mook just shook his head. "No, but I saw something even greater," he said. "Although it was like a dream."

He rubbed his face again.

"Can I *really* see you?" he asked.

"Yes, you can," they all assured him.

And Mook just smiled again.

"That is very good," he said, sitting up. "I am very glad my eyeballs did not fall out."

seven ✈

ONE HOUR AFTER BUD LEFT FOR THULE
aboard the navy helicopter with the two bags of body
remains, Mac found herself walking down one of the
Immaluost facility's long tubular hallways.

This one was known as Eight South. There were many
signs along the way. Arrows pointed directions this way
and that. Warning signs read DON'T TOUCH THIS, DON'T
TOUCH THAT. NO FOOD ALLOWED. NO DRINKS. NO SMOK-
ING. NO BREATHING. . . .

All the signs were printed in the twisted letters of
Cyrillic. To the untrained Western eye, the words
seemed intentionally jumbled up and misspelled. Plus,
all the signs were too big, too wordy, too much in-your-
face. Their combined message was clear: you were now
passing into the Russian "sector" of the Immaluost research facility. If you didn't speak Russian, then it was
going to be a difficult journey.

Luckily, Mac spoke Russian.

She reached a set of office doors and found the one
she was looking for: Dr. Marina Spokosvitch.

Mac knocked once and got no reply. She knocked
again, a bit harder, the noise echoing up and down the
rounded hallway. Still nothing. She tried the door. It was

unlocked. She carefully turned the knob and let herself in.

At first Mac thought the woman behind the desk was dead. She was leaning far back in her battered office chair, head tilted oddly to one side, eyes open, staring straight ahead. Her mouth was open, with a bit of moisture at the corners. Not drool, Mac realized quickly. Tears, running down her cheeks.

Mac stepped in and cleared her throat and made her presence known. The woman behind the desk was not startled—she just looked at Mac and smiled sadly. Her face was as white as a corpse. Only the tears running down her cheeks seemed real.

"Dr. Spokosvitch?" Mac asked gently. "Are you all right?"

The woman of about forty-five turned slightly and nodded.

"Just remembering an old friend," she said in heavily accented English.

Mac took another step forward. The small office was a clutter of books, computer printouts, used coffee cups, arctic weather gear, Russian and British magazines, and ashtrays—ashtrays everywhere, all of them overflowing. Yet the air smelled not of cigarette smoke, but of flowers and perfume.

"I am Major Sarah Mackenzie," Mac said, taking one more step forward. "I believe you were expecting me?"

The woman turned around in her chair to face Mac. She looked her up and down twice and then motioned her forward.

"Yes, please sit down," she told Mac finally. "You look tired, my dear. Are you?"

Mac was thrown for a second by this comment. Did she really look that bad? Or was it just a small chess move on the part of the Russian doctor? Mac knew it was the Russian way, in fact almost routine, to throw a curve ball in an effort to get an upper hand when first meeting anyone viewed as a contemporary.

"Not at all, I slept half the way up here from Maryland," Mac replied. "I'm surprised how comfortable our air force cargo planes really are."

The doctor smiled a bit—Mac translated this to mean, "touché."

"Well, perhaps I will ride in one of your comfortable military jets someday," she said with a bit of a laugh.

Mac moved some computer printouts and sat down across the chaotic desk from Spokosvitch.

"I've come to ask you some questions about Sergei . . . and his death," Mac began. "I've been asked along with two colleagues to look into the matter. Tragic as it is—"

The doctor laughed. "Tragic?" she said, the faraway look returning to her eyes. "Do you Americans really know what *tragedy* is?"

Mac leaned back and smiled. "I'm sure in our own way we do," she said. "But with Sergei may I ask: were you close?"

Dr. Spokosvitch's face dropped a bit.

"Very close," she replied. "Very . . ."

"When was the last time you saw him?"

The doctor looked at her hands—they were red, raw, the hands of a working person.

"An hour before he went out onto the ice for the last time," she said. "Perhaps two."

"What was his demeanor," Mac asked, going down the list of questions she'd set into her memory. "Happy? Sad?"

"He was Sergei," Spokosvitch replied. "He was neither happy nor sad at different times. Rather he was happy *and* sad always at the very same time. That's what made his character."

"Did you know of any relationship he had with Lieutenant Lapkin?" This was an important question.

Spokosvitch laughed. "You really don't know much about Sergei, do you?"

Mac shrugged. "That's what I'm here for. . . ."

"It's safe to say that Sergei had a relationship with *everyone* at this place," she said.

Mac's eyebrows went up a bit.

"Everyone?"

"*Da* . . . ," Spokosvitch replied staunchly.

Mac's eyebrows never really came back down.

"That's a lot for one person to spread around," she said.

"Not for a person such as him," Spokosvitch replied. "He was a unique individual. A pure Russian, as we called him. Rumored to be descended from the czars. He was cultured. Well-read. Sensual . . ."

She stared at the ceiling for a moment. Mac remained silent.

"Sergei was an intoxicating individual," the Russian went on. "He would intoxicate the men with his intellect. He would intoxicate the women with his . . . well, let us just stay polite and say, his 'other talents.' "

Mac nearly laughed. This was not what she'd expected from the good doctor Spokosvitch.

Spokosvitch saw her expression and laughed herself. "Now you are getting a glimpse of Sergei."

"Was it like him to go out onto the ice so unprepared?"

Spokosvitch just shrugged.

"I saw him once go out with no clothes on," she said. "That was a wonderfully mad moment."

"So . . . what are you saying, exactly?"

Spokosvitch shrugged again. "If the mood struck Sergei, anything was possible."

Mac took a moment. The next question was the most important.

"He seemed like such a popular fellow," she began. "Do you know anyone who would want to see him dead?"

Spokosvitch laughed again.

"Yes," she said in English, but no less firmly.

Mac leaned forward a bit in her chair. "Who? Who wanted to see him dead?"

Spokosvitch looked around at all the filled ashtrays. Then tears began to form again in her eyes.

"Everyone," she said again, finally, with a long sigh. "Simply everyone. . ."

eight ✈

AT THAT SAME MOMENT, HARM WAS AT THE opposite end of the research station, bored to death.

He was sitting in an office located in tube Six North. It was the exact same size as the office belonging to Dr. Spokosvitch, but they might as well have been on different planets.

Or make that, different galaxies.

This office was pristine, regimented. Books stacked in alphabetical order on neat shelving covered one wall. Computer printouts standing at attention in a glass case guarded another. Outer-weather gear hung, prim and proper, in a small handmade walk-in closet near the door. The room smelled of oak, furniture polish, cheap leather, and burnt tea. No cigarette butt had ever been crushed out in this place. In fact, no cigarette, lit or otherwise, had ever even made it through the door.

This was the office of Dr. Jerome Heidkamp, the scientific leader of the mission at Immaluost Station. Harm had been sitting here, captive for the past thirty minutes, listening to Heidkamp lecture him on the importance of ice. Blue ice. Green ice. Summer ice. Winter ice. Ice cubes in your drink. Ice cubes in your bath. And most especially, arctic ice, the very best of which could be found right around Immaluost Station.

"I cannot emphasize the importance of the ice pack up here," Heidkamp was saying to him now, adding without a trace of irony, "and I truly believe that if it weren't for all this beautiful ice, none of us would be here at all."

"Well, you've probably got a point there," Harm told him.

As Heidkamp droned on about referential ice pressures and saturated salt packs, Harm tried his best to get a full measure of the man. Heidkamp was a civilian and it was obvious that he considered his scientific status to be of far greater importance than any military rank. For example, there was no American flag in his office, no mandatory presidential photograph. No indications at all that he was working at a *military* research station.

Heidkamp seemed to be one of those academic types who, good, bad, or indifferent, wore everything right out there on his sleeve, his unquestionable intelligence blinding him to the real world. Harm was sure it had never dawned on the sixty-ish, goateed doctor that only ice-core specialists would consider a posting to Ice Station I'm Lost to be a plum assignment. If he only knew of the unhappiness with which the regular navy personnel viewed their appointment to this windswept and unwelcoming place, he'd probably be bowled over.

Or then again, Harm thought, maybe he wouldn't really give a damn.

"As far as I'm concerned, it is the duty of the navy to serve science," Heidkamp was suddenly saying to him, as if he'd read his exact thoughts. "In fact, in anything short of war, what reason is there to have a navy except to make things easier for people who have more important things to do? The work that my team is doing here will end up benefiting all of mankind in the end— not just the navy.''

Harm just nodded as if he gave a rat's patoot. Despite the nonstop lecture, he was being punctiliously polite to the man. And though Heidkamp's brusque manner was trying on his good manners, it didn't matter. Harm could be counted upon to be polite to a vulture if the situation called for it. Working in JAG did that to a person.

Finally Heidkamp took a breath.

"So then, do you know why I'm here, Doctor?" Harm asked him quickly.

"Of course I do, Commander," Heidkamp replied. "You want to know what the death of Sergei means to my team. Well, I'll tell you: simply put, we have one less scientist on board. I regret the death of Lieutenant Lapkin as well, although I did not know her. In any case, what has happened has happened. What I need to know from you is what does this mean to the overall mission? Is there any danger that the military authorities will intervene? Pull the plug up here?"

Harm just stared back at the man. He couldn't believe someone so smart could be so off the beam. Or was he just being cagey?

"I'm here as part of the investigation of these deaths, Doctor," he finally replied. "I have no idea how it will affect your funding or your research."

Heidkamp looked back at Harm strangely.

"Investigation?" he asked. "They were eaten by polar bears, horrible creatures that they are. I don't know a damn thing about them, other than that they apparently eat anything that moves, including humans. But beyond that, what's to investigate?"

Harm leaned forward and fixed his gaze on the scientist.

"Sergei Bodachenko was a friend of yours, wasn't he? As well as being a collaborator on this project?"

Heidkamp nodded. "I did know him well. Truly. . ." There was a spark of genuine sorrow in Heidkamp's voice.

"Ever get any indication that he might have been romantically involved with Lieutenant Lapkin or any one else?"

Heidkamp seemed embarrassed by the question. "I know that Sergei had more than a passing interest in— how shall I say it—'prolific' sex. He talked about it a lot. Too much, in fact. But beyond that, I haven't the foggiest idea if they were an item."

"Do you know anyone who would want to do either of them harm?"

Heidkamp seemed stunned by this question—either that, or he was a good actor.

"Do you mean cause physical harm?"

"Exactly," Harm replied.

Heidkamp pulled nervously on his tiny white beard.

"Not really," he finally replied. "He was a peach of a guy, and she was so pretty . . . or so I've heard."

Heidkamp lowered his voice and leaned a bit toward Harm.

"But why do you ask?" he spoke with a dramatic whisper, "Surely you can't think this was anything more than an accident."

Harm just shrugged. "I have to consider all possibilities," he said. "It's my job."

Heidkamp mulled this over for a moment, then pounded his desk for emphasis and said, "As do I. In my line of work, it's especially important to try to cover all angles. Take, for instance, what we call up here 'violet ice.' . . ."

Harm was spared another lecture by the timely ringing of Heidkamp's phone. The doctor picked up and immediately launched into another esoteric conversation with the poor soul on the other end. The topic, of course, was ice.

This gave Harm the opportunity to jump out of his chair, zip up his briefcase, and put on his hat. He couldn't get out of this place fast enough. Heidkamp was either the most arrogant man at the top of the world, or the most absentminded. Either way, Harm could simply take no more of him. So by the time Heidkamp had abruptly hung up the phone, Harm was ready to go.

"Thanks for your time, Doctor," he said. "If I need anything else, I'll give you a holler."

"Glad to help," Heidkamp replied. He wasn't getting up; instead he was dialing his phone, apparently to bore someone else.

So Harm showed himself to the door. And it was here, on the side of the homemade winter-gear closet, that he saw something that would prove very puzzling.

It was a photograph, framed nicely and hanging at eye level. It showed two polar bears, standing on their hind legs, looking down on the Immaluost Station from a nearby hill. It was almost as if they were casing the joint for a break-in. Just how the photographer had been able to get such a close shot, Harm could not tell—a super-powerful zoom lens was really the only way.

But it was the inscription in the photo's lower-right-hand corner that caught his attention.

It read,

Dear Doctor, I know how much you like our furry neighbors. Looks like a mother and her cub, doesn't it? Enjoy!

It was signed,

Your favorite nurse, Stacy.

nine ✈

"*WHERE DID YOU EVER GET A SHIRT LIKE* that?"

Bud look down at his now-very-wrinkled Hawaiian shirt and sighed heavily.

"It's really a very long story, sir," he replied.

The air force flight surgeon looked at him and said, "It better be. As a physician, I'd recommend counseling for anyone I knew wearing a shirt like that, especially up here."

This conversation would have been bad enough—the fact that it was taking place inside a morgue made it all that more displeasing to Bud's stomach.

Before him, laid out on a large, stainless-steel table, were the frozen remains of what were once two human beings.

Bud hated to admit it, but they looked like something more readily found in a butcher's freezer.

Yet he knew they would somehow manage to occupy his nightmares for years to come.

The air force doctor, Captain Mark Robeeno, was turning over the remains as if they were nothing more than pieces of chuck, ready to be ground up. Bud had been watching him do this for nearly a half-hour now, and he really didn't know how much more of it he could take.

The flight back to Thule had been uneventful, thank goodness. Though he could tell that just about everyone he came in contact with on the air force base was trying to give him a wide berth, he wasn't sure why. Was it because he was walking around in such a loud shirt? Or had someone painted the words "navy squid" on his back? Or was it that everyone knew he was the guy who had arrived escorting several pounds of sliced-and-diced human?

Whatever the case, he'd been treated courteously if coolly. The air force had agreed to perform a quick study on the remains simply to confirm the means of death only after getting an order to do so from someone back down in Washington. Bud suspected Admiral Chegwidden had twisted yet another arm, pushed yet another button to get the thing done and to bring his three wayward lawyers back home where the temperature rose above zero on occasion.

Or at least Bud *hoped* those were the admiral's motives.

So the air force had agreed to look at the body parts and now, Bud was waiting anxiously for Captain Robeeno to pronounce cause of death as the munching of one large white furry animal—and be done with it.

But then again, why did Bud think he was suddenly going to get that lucky?

"Polar bears?" Robeeno was saying, looking over one of the larger pieces with a huge magnifying glass. "Who's theory of death was that?"

Bud just shrugged. "I don't know, sir," he said. "Someone up at Immaluost, I guess."

The air force doctor looked over at him. "Was he wearing a shirt like yours?" he asked.

Bud gulped. What was the penalty for making a false official statement?

"No, he wasn't, sir," he mistated the facts, anyway. "I mean, I'm not sure. . . ."

"Well whoever the hell he was," Robeeno said, "he was wrong."

Bud's heart sank to his feet. There would be no quick escape from this nightmare after all.

"Come over here, I'll show you," Robeeno was saying to him.

Bud gulped again and took two steps forward. Robeeno was pointing at a piece of bone.

"See that?" he said, indicating the end of the marrow-filled shaft. "That's a straight cut. No polar bear in the world could make a bite that clean. Not unless it had a perfectly squared-off set of dentures."

Bud was getting dizzy at this point.

"And look here," Robeeno was indicating another piece of bone. "That looks like an entry wound of some kind."

The doctor grabbed a powerful light and an instrument that looked like nothing less than a butcher's meat cleaver. That's when Bud closed his eyes.

A moment later he heard a clink of metal against the steel table. Then he heard it again. And again.

When he opened his eyes, he saw three mashed bullets sitting under the doctor's light.

"One question, sailor," Robeeno said with a crooked smirk. "Do the polar bears up there carry high-caliber rifles?"

Bud was staring at the trio of bullets.

"Not to my knowledge, sir," he replied.

57

"Well, then, these two met their end by means of another vicious animal," Robeeno said. "The two-legged kind."

"They were shot, sir?" Bud asked.

"Shot and then cut up—to make it look like bears were the culprits, I suspect," Robeeno said.

"Wow," Bud gasped.

"I'll write it all up for you," the doctor said. "How long are you in town?"

Bud had to think a moment. What *should* his next move be?

"I should get your report and then head back to Immaluost as soon as possible," he said. "When does the next helo flight go out? Do you know, sir?"

Robeeno just shrugged. "Well, normally I'd say they could accommodate you within forty-eight hours," he said. "But considering what day it is, I think you'll have to wait until after the golf tournament is over. I know for a fact that the helo pilots who fly the I'm Lost run are teeing off in the first group."

Bud's head was now spinning as fast as his stomach. Did he hear that right?

"Golf tournament?" he asked the doctor. "Golf—as in hitting the little white ball into a hole?"

Robeeno finished loading the remains back into a body locker, then took off his gloves and patted Bud on the shoulder.

"Well, yes, except up here we use little orange balls," he said, heading out of the morgue.

"Orange balls, sir?"

Robeeno stopped for a moment and gave Bud his crooked smile again.

"That's right, sailor," he said. "That way they don't get lost in the snow."

• • •

Bud wandered over to the Thule officer's club; he needed a chocolate milk fix in the worst way.

Both times he'd landed here—first in the big C-141 Starlifter and then in the helo ride back from Immaluost—the base had been in a down period. But now it was close to noontime, and the base was suddenly buzzing with activity.

Three C-130 Hercules cargo planes had touched down one right after the other and were now taxiing in, their huge propeller engines causing an ear-splitting racket throughout the base. Behind them, a C-2 staff jet was on final approach. Circling behind it was a C-17 Globemaster III cargo jet, and behind that, a KC-135 aerial tanker.

There was a stream of flight personnel filing into the officer's club as well; as Bud got closer he could pick out different unit patches being worn by this sudden horde of air force people. And sure enough, many were carrying golf-club bags with them.

Golf? In Greenland?

Bud knew the air force had its odd conventions; its personnel were known among the four services as the most disrespectful, most reckless, most nontraditional. And because they'd been established back in the late 1940s, they were still regarded by many as the new kids on the block.

But still—a golf tournament in the Arctic?

Bud reached the Officers Club door and went in. The place was absolutely mobbed. Once inside, many of the air force personnel had removed their flight jackets, and sure enough, many were wearing golf shirts, golf pants, and golf hats. It made for a colorful bunch; however, Bud could see nothing as wild as his own embarrassing Hawaiian shirt.

He slunk to the side of the club and worked his way through the crowd to the small food-service section. Here he retrieved two containers of chocolate milk and a chocolate-covered donut. Seeking out a corner table, he squeezed himself in between two groups of pilots.

He got only cursory glances from the air force personnel at his shirt. But not one of the pilots around him made any effort to lower their voices. And because of this, Bud unintentionally became privy to some fascinating information.

The group of air force personnel sitting to his right were wearing black flights suits—with no unit patches attached. *Special Ops*—those are the words that came to Bud's mind when he spotted the men's unusual attire. Yet because two of them were carrying bags of golf clubs, they were obviously here for the golf tourney.

"I really don't mind the ten-hour flights," one man was saying. "Looking for ghosts on the ice doesn't bother me that much. But those sixteen-hour shifts . . . my butt can't take many more of them."

"Don't worry, Eightball," one of his colleagues reassured him. "After you shoot your usual one twenty, you'll be begging to get back in that seat for the sixteen-longs."

"And that one twenty will be for just the front nine holes," a third man chimed in.

"Yuck it up, boys," the first man said. "I got one hundred bucks in my back pocket that says I top each one of you by at least one stroke—for all eighteen holes."

The two other men laughed. "That's why your butt is killing you," one said. "You've been sitting on that hundred bucks for too long."

Bud sipped his chocolate milk and munched his donut, but his ears were wide open.

The men sitting to his left were also engaged in conversation, but one that had nothing to do with betting or winter golf.

"I heard they got four solid indications last night," one man was saying. His voice, while not a whisper, was nevertheless at a guarded volume. It was only because Bud was sitting so close by that he could hear them at all.

"Where?" one of his colleagues asked.

"Same area, up near Immaluost," was the reply.

Bud's ears now went to full attention.

"Four indications? Are you sure?" the second man asked.

"Straight dilly," the first man replied. "Now correct me if I'm wrong, but they haven't got four solids in the past six weeks—never mind in one night."

"Damn," a third man breathed. "We've been flying around up there for three months—and now that it's finally time to play golf—those SOBs decide to make their move?"

"Four indications is a lot of activity, maybe the Russians finally found what we've been looking for," a fourth man said, sipping his coffee.

"Or they think *we* found what *they've* been looking for," the first man interjected.

"Well, if that's the case," the fourth man said, "and it's out to sea somewhere, then they won't need us after all. You know the orders: if it's at sea, then it's the navy's problem. Like they don't know how to drop bombs on ice."

The other three men laughed.

"Damn, if the brass hands this over to the navy," the fourth man continued, "we just might get to play our thirty-six holes then get the hell out of here. And if that happens, I never want to hear the words 'clean steel' again. Agreed?''

"Agreed," the three other men said in unison.

Bud knew it would not have been good form to start taking notes, so he tried his best to remember exactly every word he'd overheard. At first, the seemingly random statements made no sense—but Bud had a bit of James Bond in him. And he could see a pattern in the ramblings of his cross-service tablemates.

It presented a fairly screwy scenario, however. It seemed like the air force was looking for something and the Russians were looking for something, but it might not be the same thing. Or then again, it might be. And if this thing was found on land, then it was the air force's problem, but if it was found out at sea, then it was the navy's problem.

And the name of this mysterious operation was "Clean Steel." Or at least, that's what Bud thought.

He mulled all this over while draining his first container of chocolate milk and opening his second.

He needed more information, he decided. Learning just a few more things might help fit some of the key pieces together. He wanted to get a good look at the unit patch being worn by the group of men to his left, the ones hoping to dump whatever this problem was into the navy's lap.

"Can you pass the sugar please?" Bud asked the man on his left.

The pilot turned, looked at Bud for a moment, then passed the sugar shaker to him.

But then, a complication arose.

"You're not adding sugar to your chocolate milk, are you, sailor?"

Bud was stuck for a moment—but just a moment.

"No sir," he replied. Then, with an almost invisible

grimace, he shook out a small snowstorm of sugar—and covered what was left of his chocolate donut.

The man on his left was slightly horrified. "Your dentist must have a second house in Hawaii," the man said to Bud. "And he obviously sent you that shirt. . . ."

Bud just smiled and devoured what was left of his sugar-covered donut. He'd seen what he'd wanted to see. The men on his left were from the Ninety-ninth Bombardment Wing, out of Ellsworth, South Dakota. Bud knew what they flew there: B-1 bombers.

Now why would there be some B-1 bomber pilots flying way up around Immaluost, complaining about something that belonged to the navy and had something to do with bombing ice?

Bud didn't know. But if he could do a similar unit ID on the men sitting to his right, another piece might fit into place.

So he finished his tooth-decay-promoting snack and left the table. But he did not leave the club. Instead he hung around the main entrance reading a set of posters pinned to the wall near the entrance way. Indeed, a huge winter golf tournament—the Top of the World Ice Golf Tourney—was scheduled to take place near Thule Base within the next forty-eight hours. From the looks of it, dozens if not hundreds of air crews were expected to attend. There were twenty different top prizes alone.

Bud just shook his head. That was the air force for you—fly fast as hell, whine about the navy, and then play golf in the Arctic. Once again Bud was thankful that he decided to follow his father's footsteps into the navy.

He hung about the main entrance for a few more minutes before spotting his prey. The four men in the black flight suits had finished their coffee and were now heading back outside. Bud waited out of sight until they climbed into their heavy outerwear, and when they left, he followed close behind.

With the wind blowing like hell and snow squalls spiraling about the base, it was hard for anyone to detect that they were being followed. The method of bipedal transport at Thule was usually walking, head down, face turned from the wind until you bumped into something or somebody and got a bearing as to where you wanted to go. Under these conditions, tailing someone was pretty easy.

So Bud stayed close to the four men as they walked the full length of the field, winding up near a group of isolated hangars separate from the rest of the base. He slowed his pace—there really weren't that many people walking around this area and he sure didn't want to be conspicuous now. But with practiced dawdling and a convenient blow of snow, he was able to stay close enough to see exactly which hangar the men had disappeared into.

Then, once they were out of sight, Bud scrambled up to the nearest window, and by peeking through the frosted glass, saw just what kind of airplane these guys were flying.

It was a large one—a Boeing 707 frame. Bud knew this was no airliner—four big engines, lots of dull gray paint, subdued country markings, and ID numbers. A big bathtub-looking thing was hanging from its belly. This was an EC-135, a very top-secret aircraft, also known as a J-STARS.

Basically a J-STARS was a country cousin to an AWAC plane—AWACs were flying radar stations. They could comb vast areas of airspace, pinpointing enemy aircraft and vectoring friendly fighters for interceptions.

J-STARS planes did the same thing, except their eyes were focused on the ground. Watching for enemy ground movements—tanks, men, artillery—they directed ground troops or air power to these targets for quick surgical elimination.

But Bud knew there were only a few J-STARS airplanes operating for the air force and that they were very expensive to fly. If someone had asked him where was the most unlikely place he'd find a J-STARS, he would have probably said the Arctic.

Until today, that is.

But what did all this have to do with the investigation up at Immaluost?

Nothing? Everything?

Bud didn't know.

But something was telling him it was up to him and Harm and Mac to find out.

ten ✈

HARM DRAINED HIS SIXTH CUP OF COFFEE IN two hours and poured another.

He was sitting in the I'm Lost mess hall, at a corner table way in the back. Four men were sitting at the table across from him. Each was wearing a loud Hawaiian shirt, a scruffy beard, and an expression that was half boredom, half annoyance.

Harm had a notebook in front of him and more pages than not were filled with scribbling—times, names, dates.

The four men before him were the last of the American workers to be questioned. Harm had already interviewed sixteen of the research experts, each one male, each one as dour as the next.

These interviews, which had now taken up the good part of his first full day at Immaluost, had led him to several solid conclusions. One was without debate: I'm Lost Station was not a happy place. Everyone he'd talked to—with the wacky exception of Dr. Heidkamp—had not only begged to be taken out with the JAGs when

67

they finally left Immaluost, several had even offered Harm bribes to do so.

The complaints about the place were many: the food was dull, the videos sent up by the navy were dull, the people were dull. Their rooms were too hot; their rooms were too cold. They worked long hours; they didn't work enough. Heidkamp was described as everything from a tyrant to a madman to a man with an ice fetish. The prospect of yet another six months of night descending on the station was simply too much for the majority of the facility's inhabitants to take.

There was another undeniable conclusion both among the navy people and the civilian workers: Lieutenant Stacy Lapkin was adorable.

Harm purposely left all questions about the deceased nurse out of the interview until each man got through with his long list of gripes about being posted to the last place on earth. Once the bitching was done, he would simply ask the interviewee how well he knew Lieutenant Lapkin. And to a man he watched as their hard faces softened, and their eyes lit up.

"She was an angel," one man said simply.

"Like my sister, only better-looking," said another.

"The girl next door," a third told him. "Even up here."

Harm discovered quite by accident that many of the men at I'm Lost secretly carried a picture of Lieutenant Lapkin in their wallets or squirreled away in their belongings.

"The farther north you go, the prettier a woman gets," one navy man told him. "We are at the top of the world—and she was the prettiest thing around for a thousand miles."

Conversely, whenever Harm asked for opinions of Sergei Bodachenko, the respondent's demeanor changed from fond sadness to deep-seated if quiet anger.

Bodachenko was roundly despised by the Americans—but for one reason only. Of all the men stationed at Immaluost, both American and Russian, Bodachenko apparently was the only one to which beautiful Lieutenant Lapkin chose to return affection.

"Everyone knew he was a hound," one American sailor had told Harm. "A real love 'em and leave 'em type. Why she picked him—over all of us—I'll never know."

Harm sipped his coffee and then one by one summoned the last four men to be interviewed. Their responses were not different from any of their colleagues. Lieutenant Lapkin was Marilyn Monroe, a soft-porn actress, and Mother Teresa all wrapped up in one; Sergei Bodachenko was a dog, a Bolshevik lothario apparently not worth the effort the polar bears had expended in devouring him.

It almost made Harm wish that he had met this odd couple before they had died.

And that was a very strange thought indeed.

Harm was up to his eighth cup of coffee when he finally finished with his last interview.

The man sulked off and Harm dove into his pages of notes. If anything he had, in record time, completed a somewhat fascinating sociological study on what happens to normal healthy American males within a confined environment who lose their personal dream girl to a guy with a Russian accent.

Too bad Harm wasn't a sociologist.

"You look like you need a cup of coffee, sailor," a voice from behind him said.

Harm turned and saw Mac standing there. She looked

as tired and frazzled as he was. She, too, was holding a notebook nearly filled with scribbling.

"If I had another cup of coffee I think I'd still be awake when the sun comes up six months from now," he said to her.

She dumped her stuff on the table beside him and said, "I have just the cure for that."

She disappeared for a moment, coming back with two containers of chocolate milk. She set one down in front of Harm and opened the other for herself.

"Suddenly this is the drink of choice?" Harm asked her.

"It works for Bud," Mac said, taking the chair beside him.

She opened her notebook to page one then looked up at him and smiled wearily.

"Well, 'Doctor,' what conclusions have you come to?"

Harm sipped his drink.

"That's actually a very easy question to answer," he replied. "All of the Americans loved Stacy and hated Sergei."

Mac laughed suddenly.

"That's funny," she said, "All of the Russians *loved* Sergei and *hated* Stacy."

They both laughed now, Mac's tousled hair briefly touching Harm's shoulder. He felt a pleasant shiver go through him.

"God, what have we gotten ourselves into?" he asked her, still laughing.

"In my very non nonexpert opinion," Mac said giggling, "a loony bin. From the reactions I got, I'm surprised these people haven't all killed each other by now."

Their giddiness passed and Harm took a long slug on his chocolate milk.

"I'll tell you one thing," he said after a while, "That polar-bear theory is looking thinner and thinner all the time."

"I agree there," Mac said. "But what does that leave us? A murder-suicide?"

Harm just shook his head. "My gut tells me no," he said. "I mean, if that was the case, who killed whom? Lieutenant Lapkin apparently loved Sergei; he apparently desired her—when something goes wrong in that sort of situation, who shoots first?"

"And who's around to chop up the bodies afterwards?" Mac added with a grimace. "And then hide the weapons. I mean, their pistols have yet to be found, but if this is a shooting, one of those guns would almost have to be the murder weapon."

"Not necessarily," they both heard a voice behind them say.

They turned to see a very tired-looking Bud Roberts standing behind them.

Uncharacteristically, he had a cup of coffee in his hand.

"Bud . . . when did you get back?" Harm asked him.

"Just five minutes ago," he said, reaching into his pocket. "And to answer your question, Major . . . those two people weren't eaten by polar bears. They were shot, and then cut up by someone trying to cover up the crime and make it look like it was polar bears."

Harm turned around fully to face Bud.

"Really?"

Bud pulled a brief report out of his pocket. "Here's the flight surgeon at Thule's conclusions," he said. "Bottom line, they were both shot with six bullets each."

"But you said their pistols were not the weapons used?" Mac asked him, puzzled.

"No ma'am," Bud said, placing three items on the table. They were the recovered bullets.

"These were not fired from a pistol," he said. "They are high-caliber ammunition. They were fired from a high-velocity rifle of some kind, probably a military-type weapon."

Harm and Mac just looked at each other.

"Just when this thing seems like it can't get any crazier, it does," Harm said.

Bud finally slumped into the seat next to Harm.

"With all due respect, sir," he said wearily, "it's about to get worse."

They spent the next ten minutes listening to what Bud had uncovered at Thule. The mysterious air crews, the talk about some special operations going on up in the vicinity of Immaluost Station. The uneasy cooperation between the air force and navy. The snow golf tourney.

"If it wasn't for that golf tournament," Bud said, "I would never have heard any of this stuff. I'm still not sure I should even know it. Or be spreading it around."

Harm was just shaking his head.

"B-1 bombers? A J-STARS plane flying around?" he said. "Up here? Why?"

Mac could only shake her head. "It must be a separate thing from this entirely," she said. "I mean, it *has* to be. What would these two deaths have to do with a highly secret operation involving the air force, the navy, the Russians . . ."

Harm just shook his head.

"I don't know," he said finally. "But doesn't it seem like too much of a coincidence for there *not* to be a connection? I mean, we're at the top of the world here.

And suddenly it's becoming a very crowded place."

"Bud, did you happen to hear what the name of this secret operation was?" Mac asked.

It was funny because that piece of information was the only thing Bud had written down. He checked a small scrap of paper stuffed inside his jacket pocket.

"One of the people I overheard said the words 'clean steel,' " he reported.

Clean Steel?

Where had Harm heard that expression before?

He slowly sipped his chocolate milk, deep in thought.

"Do they have Internet access up here?" he asked Mac finally.

She shrugged. "I really don't know. I imagine they might."

"Bud, are you awake enough to track that down? Maybe Thorpe has a computer you can use. You can brief him on what you learned at Thule. Then, if you can get on-line, input 'clean steel' and see what you get."

Bud nodded wearily.

"Will do," he said. "But may I ask what you are planning to do?"

Harm drained the last of his chocolate milk.

"For what it's worth," he said, "I think it's time we visited the scene of the crime."

eleven ✈

IT WAS A BIT TOO WARM INSIDE COMMANDER
Jake McKinney's cabin.

He rose from his desk and its perpetual pile of paperwork and walked over to the heat control. It was set
on seventy degrees, just where is should have been. But
the thermostat was obviously off and he estimated it
might have been closer to eighty or more inside his quarters.

He loosened his tie and unbuttoned the top button of
his shirt. How ironic. He was just a few dozen miles
from the North Pole, where the average temperature outside was thirty below—and yet he was too warm.

"Not that crazy," he murmured to himself, returning
to his desk and its mountain of paperwork.

McKinney had been the CO of the *Polar Star* for
nineteen months and it might have been his best duty in
his dozen-plus years at sea. His friend Thorpe was
right—McKinney *was* made for the wild and woolly
places. And they didn't get much woollier than Immaluost Island.

But he also knew that when in a hostile environment,
being smart and consistent were the two keys for avoid-
ing disaster. Survival against such outrageous elements

could become a routine if everyone involved respected the procedures.

It was for this reason that McKinney insisted that all the members of his crew live on the *Polar Star* during its deployment to the research station. While berthing inside the station itself might have been more comfortable—certainly there would have been more room available for each individual—that was just not McKinney's idea of running things. His crew was in the service to operate and maintain its vessel. Transferring over to the station itself would leave them open to picking up bad habits. These would then lead to sloppiness and reduced vigilance. And then when disaster struck, it would hit hard.

So his men stayed here on the ship every night and drilled every day and kept the equipment in top condition and the power plants humming and *that* was the reason it was now too warm inside his cabin.

Nevertheless, he could live with it. To him, and to all onboard, the ship represented safety in a very harsh world.

As for the research station itself, well, that's where the nightmares were.

The soft rapping at his cabin door came just as McKinney finished his last piece of paperwork.

"Come," he called out, almost absentmindedly. He was sure it was one of his staff, coming to ask him some routine question.

So it was a mild surprise when he looked up to see two of his sailors flanking a third man walk through the doorway.

The third man was dressed from head to toe in seal fur. What struck McKinney first, oddly enough, was just how much this man's outfit would cost back in the real

76

world. A thousand dollars on Fifth Avenue, perhaps? The stranger was obviously one of the natives from the Ininitka tribe further up the coastline.

"Sorry to bother you, Skipper," one of his men began, "but this gentleman insisted on seeing you."

"It's not a bother," McKinney said, buttoning his shirt and redoing his tie. "Please come in . . . Mr. . . . ?"

"I am Mr. Mook," the old man said in thick but surprisingly good English. "And there is something I must tell you about. . . ."

McKinney knew a little about the Ininitkas.

They were an ancient family who had hunted whale until the Danish government halted that practice twenty years before. In return for honoring the whaling ban, the Danes gave the Ininitkas two motorized fishing boats and now the family got along by net fishing and capturing seals.

If McKinney was correct, the Ininitkas had increased in population since the switch over to net fishing. He also knew that their life span—notoriously low for the past century—had also increased in the past two decades.

But although McKinney had researched these people a bit upon first coming to Immaluost—it was in his nature to do so—he had never really met one of the Ininitkas face-to-face.

So this was an occasion.

He dismissed the two sailors and bade Mook to settle into one of the easy chairs McKinney had in his office. Mook did so, settling in slowly, as if he'd never sat on leather before, which he hadn't.

"May I offer you something to drink?" McKinney asked him.

Mook looked around the cabin. Never had he been

surrounded by so much steel and wood before.

"Do you have any black water?" he asked.

McKinney thought a moment, then pointed to his percolator.

"Do you mean coffee?"

Mook smiled and McKinney saw he had but two teeth left in his mouth: one on the top, one on the bottom.

"If that's what you call it," Mook said.

McKinney poured them both a cup, handed a mug to Mook, and then sat back down. The native was like someone from another planet. His skin was leathery and slightly orange. His eyes were wide and slightly Asian in appearance. His hair was very long, gray, and stringy. His hands looked like they could crush stone. Yet Mook was probably no more than ten years older than McKinney himself.

"I have seen a ghost ship," Mook said simply after gulping down half of his steaming cup of coffee. "I thought I should report it to you."

McKinney stopped his coffee in mid-sip.

"Ghost ship?"

Mook nodded calmly. "Yes," he replied matter-of-factly. "I encountered it yesterday, while looking for 'the lights under the ice.' I'm not sure why, but it seemed that this vision might be something that you people here would want to know about."

McKinney was temporarily at a loss for words. He wasn't expecting this.

"Tell me what happened to you, please," he finally managed to croak.

"I was out paddling in No Seals Bay," Mook began, "and this thing came up behind me. It must have destroyed my kayak because I have yet to see it again. This thing was huge and black and just how my elders described the ghost ships from old."

He took another massive gulp of coffee.

"It must have hit me very very hard, because I don't remember much after I first saw it," he went on. "My relatives found me on the beach several hours later. They thought I was dead. *I* thought I was dead. Or at least that my eyeballs had fallen out."

He finished his coffee in one last massive slurp, then said, "But here I am. Alive enough to tell you the story."

But McKinney was greatly puzzled. In all his years in the navy, he had never quite faced anything like this. He really wasn't sure what he should do.

Was this just some musing of an old man? Or had something really happened there?

"Can you describe in detail what this thing looked like?" he asked Mook.

Mook's eyes got a faraway look in them. He remained that way for a very long time.

Then he simply answered, "No."

McKinney felt the air go out of him.

"But I might be able to draw it," Mook said with a gaping smile.

McKinney immediately retrieved a pen and paper from his desk and handed them to Mook.

"Draw it," he said. "And take your time."

It was strange. When McKinney handed Mook the pen and paper and told him to draw, he thought he would be looking at a scribbled image within a minute's time.

But Mook surprised him. The native began drawing very meticulously. Five minutes turned into ten, ten into twenty. McKinney dared not look at what the native was drawing. He dared not move. His phone rang twice, but he ignore both calls. Through it all Mook just kept on drawing.

Finally, after nearly thirty minutes, his image was complete. Like an *artiste* presenting his latest masterpiece, Mook smiled and slowly turned the paper around.

"Do you recognize such a ship?" he asked McKinney innocently.

McKinney just stared at the drawing in disbelief.

"*This* is what you saw?"

"It is," Mook replied. "Is it familiar to you?"

But McKinney did not reply. Instead he just whispered, "Oh, my God . . ."

Then he got up, hurriedly dialed his phone, and barked into the receiver: "Get the security officer up here on the double."

McKinney took another look at the drawing. It was incredibly detailed, frighteningly so.

"And get me Commander Thorpe over at the station," he added. "*Immediately . . .*"

twelve ✈

THE ARCTIC CAT MADE THE TWO-MILE TRIP from the research station to the place called Lookout Point in less than twenty minutes.

The weather, while overcast, had cooperated by not blowing snow in every direction at gale-force winds. This meant the trek out to the elevated outcrop of rock and snow was not as unpleasant as it could have been. Still, due to the uneven terrain, a gradual climb, and high snowdrifts, the tracked vehicle could only move at about ten miles per hour.

Harm and Mac were in the backseat of the four-person vehicle. Thorpe was riding up front, and one of his lieutenants was doing the driving. The Cat made so much noise grinding through the densely packed snow, that conversation was nearly impossible. Harm took the time to go over his notebook full of scribbled interviews—but there were no secret conclusions to be found in the chaotic transcripts. The same was true for Mac's interviews. The international family inhabiting I'm Lost Station was as dysfunctional as any found in Middle America. If they weren't at the top of the world, they would have been perfect for the latest slugfest TV talk show.

Mac spent the trip staring out the Cat's window, almost mesmerized by the stark beauty of the vast polar landscape. It was hard sometimes to see exactly where the land left off and the sky began, and that gave one a sense of disproportion that bordered on hallucination. There were more human footprints on the moon than in this place, she thought. How strange, then, that one of the few human incursions to such a place resulted in, at the very least, two very bizarre deaths.

It's just too beautiful for that, she kept thinking over and over.

Thorpe had his driver stop about one hundred yards away from the site where the bodies had been discovered.

Climbing out of the Cat in their heavy arctic gear took some doing for polar amateurs like Harm and Mac. (Harm practically had to be pried out of the backseat.)

Once out, however, they carefully trudged through the snow to the place were three yellow and four orange markers had been hammered into the frozen ground. These were the locations of the remains: yellow for Lieutenant Lapkin; orange for Sergei Bodachenko.

They were more scattered than Harm had imagined and were not aligned in any particular way. There were no signs of blood in the ground below the markers—the snow and wind had taken care of that days ago. Nor were there any polar bear tracks in evidence. But the gale-force winds that frequently ripped across the island would have taken care of them, too.

As a result, there really wasn't much to see at the crime scene—not at first, anyway.

While Mac took pictures of the site, Harm wandered away, climbing a small bank of rocky outcrops, which led to the summit of Lookout Point. Upon reaching the top, he was somewhat surprised to see the deep-blue sea just on the other side of the icy cliff. With everything being some shade of white, it was easy to lose perspective exactly as to where one was on the island. Harm hadn't realized they were still so close to the sea.

But even more surprising was that there was a structure just on the other side of the hill, nestled in a bay, that had steep walls of ice and snow on three sides of it.

This structure was very dilapidated. It had been built of thick wooden logs and covered with tar paper. Amazingly, though it had to be at least fifty years old, the construction was holding up extremely well.

Harm took out his binoculars and studied this place. It had obviously been a facility where boats had been tended, but he could see the remains of only one very primitive dock. It appeared to be big enough to tie up a couple rowboats and no more. By comparison, the building itself was good-sized, three stories high, with a lighthouse tower on its top: way out of proportion to the size of the dock.

So what kind of boats had been served here? Harm wondered.

He studied the building a little more closely. Its design had been purely functional—a four-sided, three-level safe haven built to protect those inside against the harsh elements. It was hardly a work of architecture, then. Sturdy. No frills.

Military. . .

Harm slid back down the hill and returned to the rest of the party. Mac was still taking pictures; and Thorpe and his lieutenant were looking in every direction, M-16s in hand, watching for polar bears. Though Thorpe had been briefed on Bud's findings that the two deceased had not met their end courtesy of the wild beasts, that didn't mean there weren't any of them hanging around.

A polar bear, Harm had just learned recently, could detect a potential meal from as far as five miles away. He silently hoped now that Thorpe and his looie had properly oiled and warmed their rifles before proceeding out onto the ice pack.

He also hoped they were good marksmen.

Mac went through two rolls of film, essentially taking pictures of the indents in the snow around the yellow and orange markers. It was only by chance then that the weakened sun broke through the thick overcast for just a moment, sending a ray of light down to the ground beneath her feet. That's when she saw a glint of something located about six inches down in the snow.

The sun's ray lasted just a second, but Mac's eyes never left the spot where she'd seen the reflection. She started digging immediately and after some chipping and scraping, found what was giving off the reflection.

Harm was at her side by now.

"That's not a beer-bottle cap, is it?" he asked.

She wasn't sure herself. Her bulky gloves made the object hard to handle. But finally she was able to get it between two fingers. It was a piece of metal—tubular, bent, and battered.

"Shell casing," she said, almost out of surprise than anything else.

Harm examined it, nearly as surprised as she.

"Wow, what a find."

She held it up to her eyes and saw that their luck was getting even better. There was some inscription on the bottom of the casing. But because the shell had been fired, ejected, and then crushed somewhat in the ice, the lettering was nearly indecipherable to the naked eye. But a few letters could be seen, and one thing was clear—they were not English.

"Is that . . . is that what I think it is?" Harm asked.

"Russian lettering, you mean?" Mac replied. "It could be."

Thorpe had joined them by now, and the three of them began digging in circles radiating out from where the shell was found. But no more little treasures could be found.

"If we get that back to the research station we can put it under a microscope, I'm sure," Thorpe said.

"A magnifying glass might even do," Mac said.

Harm detected some worry in her voice. "That's a key piece of evidence," he said to her after Thorpe went back to retrieve his lieutenant. "It fits Bud's information that these people were killed by a high-caliber weapon. You don't seem too happy about finding it."

Mac still had the shell up to her eyes, trying to make some sense of the battered lettering.

"Well, suppose this is Russian writing, what does it give us, really?" she asked.

Harm just shrugged. "It means we probably narrow down the number of suspects by half," he said. "And to me, that means we are halfway to the end of this bad dream and that much closer to taking a silver bird out of here."

"And what if it *isn't* Russian in origin?" she asked cryptically.

But Harm had already moved away and didn't hear her. He was running after Thorpe.

Mac continued to study the shell, as if the longer she looked at it, the more likely the battered lettering would make some sense. But she had no such luck now.

It would have to wait until they returned to Immaluost Station.

Mac found Harm and Thorpe again, standing atop the ridge looking down to the bay below.

They were discussing the old wooden building Harm had discovered close to the edge.

"Believe it or not," Thorpe was saying, "the Germans built it during the Second World War. It's an R and P station."

"Refueling and provisioning?" Harm guessed.

"That's right," Thorpe confirmed. "They built it in 1941, after they overran Denmark. Seeing as Greenland is a Danish possession, I guess the Nazis thought they'd inherited it. From what I understand, a German naval contingent just showed up here one day, built this place, left a couple dozen people to run it. They serviced a squadron of U-boats used to raid convoys heading for Murmansk.

"When things went south for the Nazis, they bugged out—this is all that remains."

On a nod from Harm, Mac began snapping pictures of the place.

"Actually, there's a little piece of history associated with this place," Thorpe went on. "It's the site of one of the few victories of the Danish Navy over the Germans."

"Really?" Harm and Mac asked at the same time.

"The story goes that one of the U-boats came limping up here and met a Danish patrol boat of some kind about a mile out. The sub couldn't dive for some reason, and the Danes had a bigger deck gun than they did. They traded shots for about a half-hour and finally the Danes nailed the U-boat's forward magazine. The sub went down in about a minute, I was told. No survivors . . . a clean shot to the bottom. . . ."

Clean? the word went through Harm's mind again. *Clean steel?*

He'd heard that term before—but where? And what did it mean?

"The natives further up the coast really hate the fact that there's a sub on the bottom out there somewhere," Thorpe went on, almost as an afterthought. "They're convinced that if you go into the cold drink alive, then the ice spirits will preserve your body—you know, for thawing out later."

"Flash-frozen ghosts?" Harm said with a chuckle.

Thorpe just shrugged, staring out at the vast ice, smooth as a mirror ocean.

"Something like that, I guess," he finally said.

That's when they heard the unmistakable growl of the Arctic Cat's engine being revved up. They all turned to see Thorpe's lieutenant waving madly for them to return to the snow vehicle.

All three went sliding down the hill and ran awkwardly to the vehicle. The lieutenant was on the Cat's radio, but it was obvious he was having trouble talking to someone on the other end.

"What's up, bubba?"

The young navy officer just shook his head slowly. "I just got the craziest call from base," he said.

"Crazy, how?" Thorpe asked him.

"It was someone who's voice I didn't recognize telling us we better get back to the station immediately," he reported. "They said things were out of control. . . . and that 'the sea had turned red.' Then they just hung up. Now I can't raise anyone down there. I get no reply on either wave band."

Harm and Mac and Thorpe all just looked at each other.

" 'The sea has turned?' " Harm said. "Is that some kind of code, Commander?"

Thorpe was shaking his head vigorously. "It's not in any code book I'm privy to," he said.

He gave the lieutenant a nod and the man jumped

back behind the Arctic Cat's wheel and revved the engines again.

Then Thorpe turned back to Harm and Mac. His face was a mix of bafflement and concern.

"Climb aboard," he told them urgently. "We've got to get back there as fast as we can."

thirteen ✈

IT TOOK ONLY ABOUT HALF THE TIME TO RE-
turn to Immaluost Station as it had to drive out to the
crime scene.

With his CO's permission, Lieutenant Bubba had applied full power to the huge arctic vehicle and all four
of them were astonished how fast the thing could go
when worrying about a blown engine and twisted transmission was not a priority.

Once again talk inside the cabin was impossible during the ride back. This just made it even more unnerving
for them, with all of the wildest ideas and possibilities
of disaster flying through their heads. Though obviously
worried, Thorpe stayed cool. He methodically kept trying to raise the station on the radio, but with no success.

Harm and Mac were thus left to their own disturbing
theories—their main concern was whether Bud was all
right.

Finally they were rolling up the side of the hill that
looked down on the station. Thorpe was practically up
out of his seat edging for the first glimpse of his little
kingdom, the uncertainty of what had befallen it charging through his bones.

Bubba gave the throttle one last goose and they finally

topped the summit. Bubba applied the brakes and the big Cat came to a snowy, wind-blown halt.

They all looked down on the research station and gasped.

"Well, I'll be damned," Thorpe breathed. "The sea *has* turned red. . . ."

They couldn't believe it.

Tied up at the dock next to the USCGC *Polar Star* were three enormous Russian warships.

They made it down to the research station in just two minutes—again, record time. Thorpe leapt out of the cab even before the Cat stopped moving. Harm and Mac were right behind him.

There were blue-coated Russian sailors moving around everywhere. Some were armed, some were not. The majority of them were wrestling with an equally large group of American sailors on the large snowfield located next to the main building of the station.

Harm and Mac came to a sliding halt and watched in amazement at the brawl that was going on in the center of the facility. There were at least thirty people from both sides involved and it was nothing less that hilarious to see grown men in huge heavy arctic parkas trying to land punches on each other.

But then Mac spotted something even more outrageous. Battling fiercely somewhere near the middle of the pile of flying arms and legs was one familiar face.

"God, is that who I think it is?" Harm asked incredulously.

It was Bud.

There were people on both sides of the fight trying to break it up. Dark-coated Russian officers were pulling their men off, and American scientists and navy personnel in orange exposure suits were doing the same thing.

Harm ran forward and managed to drag Bud out from the bottom of the pile.

The feisty junior officer landed three successive blows on an equally red-faced Russian ensign before Harm was finally able to extract him from the fray.

Finally peace was being restored to the center yard. Suddenly Thorpe was at the center of things.

"Stand down!" he screamed.

Several of his junior officers came forward and stood at attention—this also looked very funny in heavy winter gear.

Thorpe went right up into the face of his second-in-command, a normally sunny African American, Lieutenant Charlie Spring.

"What in God's name is going on here?" Thorpe growled at him.

Spring's eyes never diverted from looking straight ahead.

"I was awakened by the messenger of the Watch, sir, to find that these—well, these visitors—were in violation of a security list, sir."

Thorpe looked at his ragged, snow-packed sailors. "So you started a fist fight?" he roared at Spring.

Spring finally broke rank. "*They* started it, sir!" he yelled, pointing at the equally snow-encrusted group of Russians.

Thorpe didn't know whether to laugh or cry. He looked over at Harm and Mac who were, without a doubt, laughing.

Thorpe just shook his head. "Mister Spring, call your troops together, go inside, and get to your quarters. You will wait there until I have enough time to deal with you."

"Yes, sir!" Spring cried.

With that, all of the American personnel sullenly filed

back into the living quarters building. To Harm and Mac, they looked like a line of defeated penguins.

Thorpe then turned to the senior American scientist. He was a mousy kind of guy named Porter.

"Doctor, would you happen to know where the commander of those ships is?"

Porter stepped forward. You could tell by the expression on his face that he wasn't too keen about giving Thorpe his answer.

"Commander Thorpe," he said at last, "I believe the Russian CO is relaxing in your office."

Thorpe's face turned beet red. He twirled around, nearly slipping on the ice, and charged into the administration building.

Harm and Mac were trying their best not to laugh— but it was hard to do.

"That guy was right," Bud was saying, "the Russians started this whole thing. They barged in here like they owned the place."

"Well, they do own half of it," Harm told Bud. He'd never seen the young officer so wound up.

"It must have been the coffee I had," Bud said, seemingly reading Harm's thoughts.

They suddenly became aware that several Russian officers were closing in on them.

"Lets go find a safe place to talk," Harm suggested.

Five minutes later they were inside Mac's quarters.

These were located in tube Four East, a place that was very isolated from the rest of the station. It was here they thought they had the best chance to talk in private. Still they kept their voices very low.

"Why are the Russians here, sir?" Bud wanted to know first off.

"They were invited here," Harm told him. "By

Thorpe—to help in the investigation. Though I doubted he expected half the Russian navy.''

"Actually, it was two cruisers and an icebreaker," Bud told him.

Harm just rolled his eyes. Bud was efficient, that much was certain.

"Look at it this way," Mac said. "Twenty years ago that fistfight would have been a gun battle. We've at least progressed that far.''

"Well, that doesn't mean we have to play footsies with them, though," Harm said.

He had a long history with dealing with Russians. He thought it was always best to be cautious around them.

"Especially after what we found up on Lookout Point near the crime scene," he added.

Bud's ears perked up and they quickly briefed him on the recovered shell casing, as well as the old German U-boat station.

Mac showed Bud the shell casing but they still could not decipher or even identify the writing on its bottom.

"There's plenty of Russians here now that would probably figure that out for you," Harm said ironically.

"I think the best thing we do with this is keep it under wraps," Mac replied. "At least until we see just what is happening here.''

She put the shell casing back in her pocket.

Harm turned back to Bud.

"Did you get anything on 'clean steel'?''

Bud just shook his head. "I was able to get on a computer but by the time the modem connected, the Russians had landed. I thought it was best to let it go for the moment," Bud replied.

"A wise choice," Harm agreed.

Harm checked the door; no one was in the hall listening in.

"What are all these Russians doing here, though?" Mac asked. "I'm sure Thorpe wasn't expecting three warships to show up."

"I agree," Harm said. "That's why I think there's a lot more to this than meets the eye."

"What do you mean?" Mac asked.

Harm returned to where they were sitting. "Well, from what we know of the Russian navy these days, three-quarters of it is sitting in port, rusting away. Thorpe gives someone here the okay to let Russians up to investigate and two capital warships and an ice breaker show up?"

"Does seem very unusual," Mac agreed. "And very fast for the Russian navy."

They were silent for a moment.

"Unless . . . ," Harm began.

"Unless they were already in the area," Mac finished for him. "And they are the Russians that Bud overheard those air force pilots talking about."

Harm thought a long while. "I think that is a distinct possibility," he said finally. "Either that or this place suddenly got very popular as a tourist attraction."

Bud looked like he was about to burst.

"There was one other thing, sir," he said. "Right before the Russians came in, Commander Thorpe got a very urgent call from Commander McKinney aboard the *Polar Star*."

"Urgent as in how?" Harm asked. "Had he spotted the Russians coming in?"

Bud just shook his head. "Nope—it wasn't about the Russians. He wanted the security officer to get up to his quarters ASAP. Something to do with one of the native people. There's a family of them that live up north along the coast. One of them was in McKinney's cabin."

"And he called the security officer?" Harm asked.

Bud just nodded. "Strange."

Harm thought for a moment. "You know this place is now so lousy with Russians, Thorpe will take hours sorting it all out."

Mac eyed him. "What are you thinking?"

Harm smiled slyly and checked the door again.

"I think we should pay a visit to Commander McKinney."

Fourteen ✈

HARM AND MAC FOUND TWO GUARDS WAIT-
ing for them at the gangway leading up to the *Polar
Star*.

With the sudden arrival of the Russian "investiga-
tors," it was obvious that some security measures had
gone into effect around Immaluost Station, and the en-
tryway to the navy icebreaker was no different.

"Is there any worse duty than standing a guard shift
at forty below zero?" Harm asked Mac as they approached.

"I don't know," Mac answered dryly. "I've been in
some courtroom battles against a certain JAG lawyer
that were so trying, I think I might have preferred standing out in the arctic cold."

"I'll take that as a compliment, Major," Harm told
her with a smile.

Mac replied with perfect timing, "And who said I was
talking about you, Commander Rabb?"

Harm just laughed, allowing a cloud of condensation
to shoot out of his mouth.

They finally reached the icebreaker's gangway. The
two sailors, their faces nearly hidden beneath their heavy
outerwear, were doing their best to stay both alert and

warm. They were armed; both men had shoulder holsters in full view. But on closer inspection, their firearms turned out to be only flare guns, the less lethal weapon of choice at Immaluost Station. The reason for this was clear: while the icebreaker's captain wasn't taking any chances in the suddenly tense climate, the last thing he wanted was an accidental shooting of some kind. So, for this frontline duty, flare guns would have to do.

Harm and Mac went through the formalities of showing their IDs to the pair of frozen sailors, who let them through promptly. Walking up the gangway, they could see other sailors manning outside positions all over the ship. They weren't posted to battle stations per se. Although the *Polar Star* had several 50-caliber machine guns and a small 40-mm grenade launcher on the stern, having them manned in face of the sudden Russian arrival might have seemed a *bit* too threatening. However, it was obvious that more members of the crew were outside on deck, mulling around, trying to keep warm, than would be considered normal. Obviously, Commander McKinney was walking a political tightrope when it came to securing his ship.

Harm and Mac made their way into the main deck passageway, where it was quite warm. They were able to remove their outer gear and stow it in temporary lockers installed just for that purpose. From here they climbed up to the one deck, arriving in a passageway located just behind the vessel's bridge. Here they found Commander McKinney's cabin. A lieutenant and two armed sailors were on duty outside his door, and unlike their frozen brethren outside, these three were carrying fully loaded M-16s. The message here was as clear as the one outside: if any unwanted visitors aboard the icebreaker made it this far, they might find more than a self-propelled flare coming their way.

Harm asked permission for him and Mac to see Commander McKinney. The lieutenant checked their IDs and then disappeared behind the cabin door.

He returned a few seconds later.

"The skipper said you can go right in," the lieutenant reported. "It's standing room only, though."

Harm and Mac walked in, and indeed found that the cabin was curiously crowded.

McKinney himself was there, of course, as was a member of his staff. He was Lieutenant Ryan Santoro, security officer for the *Polar Star*.

There were three others sailors inside the office as well as a chief. All were toting weapons. They were manning a long-range radio receiver set up against the far wall of the cabin. It was clearly marked SECURE TRANSMISSIONS ONLY—SCRAMBLER IN EFFECT. Obviously these men were here to send and receive sensitive radio messages, bypassing the usual route through the ship's radio shack. Again, this was another security measure instituted by McKinney in light of the arrival of the Russian ships.

But it was the three people sitting in front of McKinney's desk whose presence here seemed most unusual. It was accurate to say that both Harm and Mac were very surprised to see at least two of them.

Sitting in the chair closest to the door was Dr. Spokosvitch, the station's premier Russian female scientist. Next to her was Dr. Oblomov, the head of the entire Russian scientific team. In the chair next to him was a grandfatherly man dressed in a thick black sealskin suit, with long hair and wearing a wide grin. He was drinking a huge mug of scalding coffee, taking massive sips with long and noisy abandon.

Harm and Mac saluted McKinney whom they had met very briefly after arriving at the station. McKinney returned their salutes somewhat wearily, then took a look around the room.

"I wish I could offer you a seat," he said. "But there just aren't enough to go around."

Both of the Russian scientists seemed greatly embarrassed to be found here—and Harm had to admit it was the last place he'd expect to see them.

"We don't want anything to do with *them*," Spokosvitch said, obviously referring to the recent influx of fellow Russians.

"I reported what happened here to my superiors on the okay from Commander Thorpe," Oblomov explained. "Little did I know those fools in Moscow would divert three warships here. Believe me, I don't want them poking around in our affairs here any more than you Americans do. Frankly, I'm a bit frightened of them."

"As am I," Dr. Spokosvitch echoed.

McKinney just smiled. "So they came here," he said dryly.

The third visitor seemed oblivious to everything happening around him. He was simply drinking his hot cup of coffee, nodding and smiling, as if he were in the midst of some imaginary conversation. He was obviously from the native island settlement further up the coastline.

"Can we talk, Skipper?" Harm asked McKinney, who was pouring out more coffee to his trio of guests. While McKinney was trying hard to play the gracious host, especially to the Russian scientists, it was obvious that McKinney wished he was someplace else.

"Talk? Yes, I would like that," he quickly answered Harm.

He turned to Santoro, the security officer, and handed him the coffeepot. "Hold down the fort, will you, Lieutenant?"

The younger officer just gulped. "I'll try, sir."

McKinney then whispered to him, "If the Russians want to leave at any point, don't get in their way. But make sure Mr. Mook stays put, capeesh?"

"Got it, sir," Santoro replied.

McKinney, Harm, and Mac exited the crowded cabin and made their way down to the officers' wardroom.

The place was conveniently empty. A pot of coffee stood warming in the corner.

McKinney poured out three cups, something he'd been doing a lot lately. "I'll never undertip a waitress again," he said with a mock frown.

They sat at a table near the door. McKinney took a sip of his coffee and then let out a long, tired breath.

"I volunteered for polar duty to get *away* from all the hubbub," he said. "Now, suddenly, this place is like Grand Central Station."

Harm and Mac both smiled.

"You know what they say about the military," Harm said, "never volunteer for anything."

McKinney chuckled but then turned serious with his next swig of coffee.

"Well, I'm actually very glad you came over," he said. "I've just become privy to a rather mysterious piece of information that I know I just have to share with somebody—and it looks like you two are it. Are you ready to have your socks knocked off?"

"Always," Harm replied with a grin.

"You both have top-secret security clearance, I assume?"

Both Harm and Mac nodded.

With that, McKinney reached inside his jacket pocket

and came out with a meticulously folded piece of paper.

"You saw the native Ininitka in my office?"

"How could we miss him?" Mac replied.

"Exactly," McKinney said. "Well, he came down to see me earlier in this very crazy day. And he had quite a story to tell."

"We heard rumors to that effect," Harm told him.

McKinney then proceeded to brief them on Mook's tale of searching for the lights under the ice only to encounter a huge "ghost ship" which had nearly killed him.

"Now, usually I would have dismissed all this as fanciful notions on the part of our indigenous brethren," McKinney said. "But judging by all the odd stuff that's been happening up here recently, well, I thought I'd let it go one more step."

"Ghost ship, eh?" Harm said. "Well, the way things are going, I wouldn't be surprised if we started seeing UFOs."

Mac suddenly grabbed his arm. "Be careful what you wish for," she warned him.

"That's exactly how I feel," McKinney said.

They all took a sip of coffee. Mac unhooked her fingers from Harm's arm.

"In any case," McKinney went on, "I asked Mr. Mook if he could draw me a picture of what this ghost ship looked like. He agreed. Now, to be truthful with you, I expected him to scribble out something a fourth-grade kid would laugh at."

"Something tells me he was a bit more artistically inclined than that?" Harm asked.

"To say the least," McKinney replied.

With that he unfolded the piece of paper on the table in front of them. It was Mook's drawing. Harm and Mac took one look at it and felt the breath catch in their throats.

It was an incredibly realistic rendering of a large, black, very unusual seagoing vessel. It was long, slightly oblong in shape, with its sides angling down into the water to produce a weird catamaran effect. It was opaque all round except for two huge green windows on its bow. In reality, it looked like nothing less than a stealth fighter, one with its wings perversely bent into pontoons.

In fact, it *was* a stealth ship: a very top-secret one called the *Sea Shadow II*. Unlike the first *Sea Shadow*, which had been a purely experimental vessel, the *SS II* was a fully operational, and heavily armed, warship that just happened to look very strange. Its weird angles and futuristic appearance were necessary, however, for they made it invisible to radar, just like its winged cousins the F-119 stealth jet and the B-2 stealth bomber.

"Now, I think you know, as I do," McKinney said, indicating the drawing, "that the *Sea Shadow II* is a very secret piece of equipment. But this is obviously what the Ininitka native saw. Look at the conning blister, for instance. The perfect proportion of the windows. The flared tail. The dampened exhaust tubes. It *has* to be it. It matches the profile exactly. The question is, why in God's name would it be floating around up here?"

Harm and Mac could only shake their heads.

"That was the reaction of my security officer as well," McKinney said. "He checked our latest security list and found nothing that indicated the stealth ship should be up here in our neighborhood—yet obviously it is. I mean, there's no way Mr. Mook could be making this up. In fact, the way I see the scenario, this ship hit him and destroyed his kayak. He believes the friendly spirits saved him, but the *SS II* crew must have fished him out of the water. How else would he have shown up on that beach, still alive? Someone had to have put him there. Which again proves to me that there's no way he can be making any of this up.''

Both Harm and Mac nodded in agreement. Then they just looked at each other for a moment. They were both thinking the same thing.

"Do you want to do it, or shall I?'' Harm finally asked her.

Mac just sat back and took a sip of her coffee. "Be my guest,'' she said.

With that, Harm briefed McKinney on what Bud had overheard at Thule air base. McKinney's eyes got wider with each mention of B-1 bombers, J-STARS airplanes, and the mysterious search being conducting by the Russians and the Americans in and around Immaluost Island.

It took a full minute for McKinney to digest this latest information.

"Damn, now I *really* can't make any sense of this,'' he said finally, with a shake of his head. "But it could be the reason why those three Russian warships got here so quickly. Maybe they weren't diverted from any far-away port at all. Maybe they were in the area already. And these days, three Russian navy ships traveling together is considered a major deployment for them. Which indicates to me that someone in Moscow is looking upon whatever the hell is happening up here with major interest.''

Mac glanced at the drawing of the stealth ship again.

"As is someone in Washington,'' she added.

They sat there stone quite for another full minute. Finally Harm broke the silence.

"Can this get any stranger?'' he asked.

Mac gasped. Again she grabbed his arm. "Will you *please* stop saying that? Every time you do, someth—''

But it was too late. Not a second later, Lieutenant Santoro burst into the officers' wardroom.

"Excuse me, sir," he said to McKinney, "but I think you'd better see this."

Santoro walked over to the nearest porthole and wiped away the frost, exposing a clear view of the outer harbor. And about one mile off shore they saw that yet another warship was steaming in.

"God, who the hell are *these* guys?" McKinney asked.

"It's the Danish navy, sir," Santoro replied. "They say they are here to help with the investigation."

Fifteen ✈

IMMALUOST STATION

BUD ROBERTS WAS GETTING HUNGRY.

When was the last time he had eaten? He thought a moment—and felt a chill go through him. *He couldn't remember. . . .*

That was not a good sign.

He rubbed his tired eyes and pondered another question: when was the last time he'd actually slept?

Again, it seemed so long ago, he couldn't remember.

He was sitting in an empty lab, hunched over a huge magnifying glass, every muscle and nerve in his neck stretched to its limit. Beneath the glass was the battered shell casing found by Major Mackenzie up at the crime scene.

It had been a very long and tiring forty-eight hours for Bud. Flying up from Thule, flying back to Thule, flying back to I'm Lost, trying to get a modem to work, then getting in a fistfight . . .

All of that had zapped his energy—and like any working engine, his body needed refueling. But he wasn't quite sure if his eating was more important than the task he presently had at hand.

107

He was using two pairs of very large tweezers, trying to straighten out the twisted shell casing to the point that the few scuffed letters on its bottom could be deciphered.

But this was proving even more difficult than first imagined. The part of the shell where the lettering could be seen had been hit by the weapon hammer, spreading it out in some places, flattening and constricting it in others. Looking at it was like trying to look at something in a fun-house mirror. The big magnifying glass both helped and hindered this as well.

He'd been at it for an hour now, and had been able to guess at only a few word fragments of the dozen or so tiny marks that could be seen on the shell.

In Bud's opinion, these fragments appeared to be Cyrillic and that meant they could be Russian in origin. But something was telling him that this was not the case. The truth of the matter was, the words *looked* Russian in some ways, but not in other ways.

So what did that mean, exactly?

Bud didn't know.

His stomach growled again and he bit his lip. Harm and Mac had been over on the *Polar Star* for more than an hour now. Would they be back soon? Should he push on with this assignment? Or would they consider it dereliction of duty if he took a break and grabbed a cup of soup from the mess hall?

He wasn't sure. But after five more minutes of peering into the big magnifying glass, trying to read the tiny letters, he felt his eyeballs start to ache.

"If I do much more of this," he murmured, "they're going to fall out."

It was a strange thought—that of his eyeballs falling out. So much so that he decided he'd better take a break before anymore strange thoughts began popping into his head. He came up with an instant plan: he would walk quickly to the mess hall, grab some soup and chocolate milk, and bring it all back here and resume his work.

Once committed to that plan, he carefully placed the shell inside his pocket, shut off the power light, and then slipped outside the lab. He began walking down the tubular hallway, heading for the mess hall, divining its location simply by sniffing the air and following where his nose took him.

He reached the mess in short order this way, but stopped just outside of the main entrance.

Something was different here.

The place was filled.

He walked in slowly. He'd half expected to find the place crowded—with Russians. But now he was surprised. Sitting at just about every table was a new influx of sailors. They were wearing bright white blouses, ties, sailors' caps, and dark-blue pants. They all looked like something out of a fashion catalog.

Bud had no idea who these new visitors were. Their presence was so unexpected, he considered not going into the mess hall at all. The place suddenly seemed very strange. It was too big to begin with, and now it was full of these new sailors. It was all very odd.

But in the end, Bud hiked up his pants, threw his chin out, and walked directly into the crowd. Fighting his way to the food line, he eventually managed to get a huge plate of food and several containers of his precious chocolate milk.

Changing plans, he sat at the last empty table in the mess, ate his meal, and watched the newcomers come and go. Finally, after hearing snippets of conversation, he realized they were Danish.

"More people," was the first thought to come to his head. "Just what we need. . . ."

He continued shoveling his food in and drinking his chocolate milk. Bud guessed correctly that offering any visiting ship's crew a meal was the politically correct thing to do in the Arctic—and now these guys were taking full advantage of the situation, just as the Russians had done before them.

Bud quickly finished his meal—he wanted to get back to the lab and the shell casing. But he was still a bit hungry. So he went up for seconds, elbowing his way through the mass of white-shirted precisely dressed sailors, and loading up on another plate.

Bud reclaimed his seat and ate some more meatloaf, mashed potatoes, greens, and beans. But now it seemed that with every bite his eyes became heavier. Then his head began to lean forward a bit. He tried to support his skull with one hand and continue to eat with the other, but this only made him sleepier.

He took out a pen and paper and, while still eating with one hand, began to print out the handful of words of the shell's casing he'd managed to read. He thought that by printing them over and over from memory, they would make more sense to him—and keep him awake as well.

But in fact the opposite was true. The more he drew the letters, the more his eyes became strained. After a few minutes, his head became even fuzzier.

Bud's hands could barely move now. He was feeling very hot. The voices around him sounded high-pitched and speeded up, as if elves were running around his feet.

He took one last bite, and then, slowly, his head drifted down to the table. It came to rest right next to his plate of food, his napkin serving as a very thin pillow.

Though he tried hard to fight it, Bud was asleep inside of ten seconds.

sixteen ✈

"**ARE YOU SURE YOU WANT TO GO THROUGH** with this?"

Mac considered the question for what might have been the hundredth time.

"Yes, I do," she finally told Harm. "I think it's the smart thing to do, considering the circumstances."

They were standing out on the rear deck of the *Polar Star*. The ship's diminutive HH-65A helo was warming up, its tiny rotor and engines making hardly any noise at all. The pilot and Mook were already strapped inside. The shaman of the Ininitkas was smiling broadly. He was about to fly like a bird, and for this reason he could barely contain his enthusiasm.

After all the craziness that had descended on the Immaluost Station, everyone involved thought it was best to get Mook back to his people. But they also agreed that his report of seeing the ultrasecret *Sea Shadow II* could not go unchecked. To Harm's thinking, all of the strange things that were happening around them *had* to have some kind of a connection to what had started out as a rather simple mysterious-deaths investigation.

Mac and McKinney saw it this way as well. That's why it was decided that someone should go back to Mook's village with him and try to look further into the matter.

That person was Mac.

She had volunteered to go, bringing with her a two-way radio, some extra heavy outerwear, and her camera, but not much else. Mook assured them all that he would take good care of her and that he would bring her out to No Seals Bay where he had seen the ghost ship. Mac couldn't imagine herself staying at the Ininitka village for more than a day. In that time, Harm was hoping things at the research station would calm down a bit.

If that was possible. . . .

So he helped Mac into the tiny chopper and secured the door behind her. The deck crewman gave the pilot his wave-off and the little aircraft began climbing straight up.

Mac looked out the window and gave Harm a sad little wave as she flew away. He made eye contact with her one more time—and that's when he felt a chill run through his bones. A very disturbing thought had some-how popped into his head: *You will never see Mac alive again.* . . .

Harm balled his fists and steeled himself as the helicopter rose swiftly and disappeared over the horizon.

No matter what happened, he vowed, that morbid intuition would *not* come true.

Harm's next stop was the office of the station's CO, Lieutenant Commander Thorpe.

With all the confusion of the past few hours, Thorpe had not been briefed on some of the latest aspects of the investigation—most especially what Mook had reported.

Though he knew that it was going to be a difficult thing to do, Harm felt it was up to him to try to get a few minutes of Thorpe's time. With this in mind, he left McKinney to baby-sit the two Russian scientists, and made his way off the *Polar Star* and back into the station.

Once inside, his first instinct was to look for Bud. But the place was in such an uproar—the halls were crowded with Russian sailors, some taking pictures, some just generally snooping around. Under these circumstances, he knew it was best to get to Thorpe first.

So he headed right for the CO's office, and just like on the *Polar Star*, he found a pair of armed sailors standing outside.

They recognized him right away.

"You sure you want to go in there, sir?" one asked.

Before Harm could ask why not, he heard a burst of laughter coming from within Thorpe's office. Then he heard the clinking of glasses, the pouring of drinks. It sounded like a party was going on inside the office, and Harm said so to the guards.

Both men rolled their eyes.

"Been like that for an hour or so," one confirmed. "The Russians are officially apologizing for the fistfight earlier today. They've admitted their men overreacted."

"To say the least," Harm said.

He knocked twice and then let himself in.

What he saw was the exact opposite of the goofy claustrophobia of McKinney's cabin. The first thing that caught Harm's attention was a big basket of bread sitting on Thorpe's desk. Beside it was a tumbler full of salt. Bread and salt—the traditional Russian greeting.

Next to the these items was a bottle of vodka, its label printed entirely in Cyrillic. The bottle was nearly empty.

There were six Russian officers sitting on one side of

the room, with two Danish officers sitting on the other. The Russians were all wearing huge Russian fur hats and very thick overcoats even though the temperature inside Thorpe's office was very high. The Danes were dressed in the natty naval blues.

While the Danes were drinking coffee, the Russians were drinking what Harm could only assume was vodka. In fact, just as he walked in, one of the Russian officers was pouring out another round of drinks—one to Thorpe included.

Harm was shocked that the station's CO would actually be drinking on the job. But he was about to get an education on just how wily Thorpe was.

Once all the drinks were poured out, the Russians lifted their glasses in a toast, then with great flourish, threw back the vodka in an eyes-to-ceiling maneuver. When they did this, Thorpe masterfully dumped his vodka into a wastebasket at his feet, but by the time the Russians were back at eye level, Thorpe was smacking his lips, as if he'd just downed another shot along with them.

That's when he looked up, saw Harm, and winked. Harm winked back and then saluted.

"Harm, old boy," Thorpe said. "Please come in. Join us."

He stood up.

"Gentlemen, this is Lieutenant Commander Harmon Rabb. He's a good friend of mine."

The six Russians looked up and saw Harm for the first time. There was a tense silence that lasted at least ten long seconds. Then suddenly all six Russians burst into laughter. They leapt from there seats and began slapping Harm on the back and pulling him to the last empty chair. Meanwhile the two Danish officers were just sitting quietly, watching the goings-on.

Harm took a seat but then whispered to Thorpe, "We should talk . . . alone."

"We will have the chance soon," Thorpe said. "I hope."

Thorpe then turned to his Russian visitors and introduced them one by one to Harm, who really didn't catch all of the gobbledygook of names and titles. He understood, however, that they were the three captains of the three Russians ships that had come into port, plus their executive officers.

Thorpe then introduced the two Danish officers who were still sitting absolutely rigid, eyes straight ahead. They looked for all the world like they wanted to be anywhere else but here.

"Commander Rabb, we were just talking about how we hope this investigation will be coming to an end very soon," Thorpe was saying.

Harm just eyed him. "Really?"

It was an odd thing for Thorpe to say—because as far as Harm was concerned, the investigation was nowhere near being completed. In fact, it had hardly even started.

"This is true," one of the Russian officers roared. "In fact"—he made a grand gesture of looking at his watch—"I expect the investigation is already completed."

Harm looked at Thorpe who could only shrug. Not a second later, there came another knock at the door. Thorpe yelled "Come!" and the door opened. Two more Russians walked in. They were in plainclothes, however.

Harm recognized this fashion statement right away. These guys were obviously from the Russian Federal Intelligence Service, the alleged successor to the KGB— "alleged" because many people both inside and outside of Russia believed that little had changed within the Russian intelligence community except its title. It was the same bunch of crude, blundering, dangerous spies that had haunted the world for the past fifty years or more.

Meet the new boss, Harm thought. *Same as the old boss.*

This pair had a hurried, whispered conversation with the three ship captains who then let out a loud whoop. One officer lunged for the vodka bottle again and poured out another round—this time excluding Thorpe. They drank quickly and then all shook hands. Then the intelligence men scurried back out the door.

"Something I should know, gentlemen?" Thorpe asked the Russian officers.

One of the captains turned to Thorpe and said, "Our investigation is complete. We have the murderers of Sergei Bodachenko and your nurse. They have confessed and now we will transport them back to Russia for trial."

Harm was shocked. So were Thorpe and the Danes.

"*Really?*" Harm asked.

The officer nodded drunkenly. "Would you like to meet the ones who have confessed—before we take them out of here, I mean?"

Harm stood up and straightened out his clothes.

"Absolutely," he said.

It was a long walk from Thorpe's office through the tunnels toward a place called Eighteen East.

This was a room that served as a kind of cultural meeting center for all the Russians at the station. A place they could go and be, well . . . *Russian.*

The small party from Thorpe's office was marching toward that location now. The Russian officers were in the lead, simply overflowing with glee at the report that their intelligence people had cracked the case in one hour, something the Americans couldn't do in many days. Right behind them were Danish naval officers, not talking, eyes still straight ahead.

Harm and Thorpe were bringing up the rear. This gave Harm the chance to brief Thorpe quickly on what Mook had seen and Mac's present whereabouts.

"The Russians are obviously up to something here," Thorpe then told him as they walked along. "Especially in light of what your guy heard down at Thule. But if they detect that we are slighting them, even in just the mildest way, it will cause a blowup that would dwarf the deaths of the two people up here. I'm walking a thin wire here—and I got to make sure none of us falls off."

"Well, if you can keep the Russians relatively sober, we might just get to the other side," Harm told him. "But what about the Danes? What is their part in this?"

"Greenland is their possession," Thorpe said with a shrug. "Their protectorate. They must have gotten wind of the deaths and scooted up here. That's just the way they are. Very protective of the people here, believe it or not. I think to a certain extent they resent our being here—along with the Russians, whom they detest, as if you couldn't tell."

They turned a corner—and were now approaching the center of the facility.

"The Danes usually have a vessel stop off here every couple of months," Thorpe went on. "But I've never been close to any of them. Personally, I think they come up here for the food. We always offer to feed them and they always seem to eat us out of house and home."

Harm thought about this for a moment. The only Danish food he could think of was blueberry Danish or maybe yogurt. Stuff that's eaten with breakfast.

"I guess you really don't see many Danish fine cuisine restaurants, do you?" he remarked.

117

"Oh, no," Thorpe said. "And do these guys love hamburgers. When I retire, I think I'll look into opening a McDonald's franchise in Copenhagen—that is, if the navy doesn't throw me out of here before my pension kicks in."

It was funny because at that moment, as if on cue, they reached the main mess hall. And sure enough the place was filled with Danish sailors inhaling as many hamburgers as the mess cooks could supply.

And it was here that Harm found Bud.

He was still at the table in the far corner, surrounded by the ravenous Danish sailors—dead asleep.

Harm momentarily diverted from his course and checked on his colleague. He was sleeping so peacefully, it seemed like a crime to wake him. Plus something told Harm that a rested Bud might be more valuable later on.

So Harm just left him there, snoring away in the midst of dozens of Danes munching hamburgers.

He was no doubt dreaming of better things.

They finally reached the entrance to Eighteen East.

Many things began flashing through Harm's mind now. Had the Russians really cracked the case? Had someone really confessed? What then did this have to do with the ghost ship and the reports Bud had brought back from Thule?

The Russian officers burst into the cultural room first, and the Danes, Thorpe, and Harm went in right behind them. To Harm's surprise, the room was crowded with people.

They were lined up against the wall, sitting at the tables, lounging on the floor. They all looked blankly at the small group of men who had walked in.

Thorpe was baffled.

"What is this?" he asked the Russian intelligence officer who had scooted ahead of the main group.

"Our suspects," the man said without a hint of irony.

Harm did a quick count. There were more than two dozen Russian men in the room.

"But which ones are they?" Thorpe asked the intelligence man.

The officer barked out a long line of Russian. Harm didn't have to speak the language to know the man had shouted: "All suspects, declare yourselves!"

And when he did, every hand in the place went up.

seventeen ✈

MAC WAS VERY WARM. SHE WAS SO WARM,
in fact, she had taken off all but her blouse and pants.

She was sitting in Mook's spacious hut. There was a
wood stove cranking out many BTUs in one corner, and
no less than seven oil lanterns were providing both light
and heat.

There were twenty-five Ininitkas crowded into the hut.
This was also raising the room temperature. They were
mostly adult men, but there were a few women and some
kids. They were all staring at Mac—a woman looking
like her didn't come through the Ininitka village too often. Their curiosity was nearly overwhelming.

Mac didn't mind the fact that she was a novelty of
sorts a bit. The Ininitka people were incredibly friendly,
very peaceful, calm, and gentle. She noticed that all of
the adults seemed to take interest in all of the village
children. The young helped the old; the old respected
the young.

A great swarm of the villagers had come out to wit-
ness Mook's triumphant return via the Dolphin helicop-

ter. Mook led them through the village like a Pied Piper. The kids sang and clapped their hands in his wake. The adults were mightily relieved to have their spiritual leader back.

The village itself was remarkably neat and well-kept, despite its fiercely isolated location. There was a stark beauty of the Arctic and Mac was coming both to appreciate it and love it with each passing minute. The village was a collection of huts—perhaps as many as three dozen—set up on an absolutely flat snow plain about one half-mile from an inlet which, in turn, flowed out into the sea.

The only modern conveniences Mac could see were a few snowmobiles, a very small generator building, and exactly one streetlight located right in the middle of the village.

No phone poles, no cable TV lines, no satellite dishes.

Mac had to admit, she preferred this scenery to her own Maryland neighborhood.

Now she was in the hut and watching closely as the villagers prepared a huge meal to be thrown in her honor.

A large barrel of fish had been brought in and Mac had watched as Mook and his various relatives cleaned what had to be at least several dozen herring, with a few large salmons thrown in as well.

It was with mixed fascination that Mac studied this cleaning process. The wood stove had a huge pot of water set on it, which was now beginning to boil. Mook and his relatives were carefully cutting open the herring with long razor-sharp knives. Once sliced, the fish's innards were removed, the white filets being casually thrown into a smaller bucket. The remaining guts—everything from the eyes to the intestines to stomachs and other various wormy-looking things—were set down carefully on a huge, flat piece of wood placed in front of Mook.

These rather disgusting parts were then further separated—all the eyes and brains went in one big pile, all the intestines and things went in another. The care with which this was being done inevitably led Mac to consider exactly what kind of unappetizing possibility was awaiting her here.

If all of those disgusting parts wound up in the boiling water, and that was the stew that was being made in her honor—well, how could she possibly refuse to eat it?

She felt a wave of nausea come over her as Mook himself started to scoop up spoonfuls of the innards.

Tossing aside all manners, she reached over and touched his hand.

"Excuse me," she said as diplomatically as possible, "but is that our dinner?"

Mook looked at her for a moment as if she was from another planet, which in some ways, she was to these people.

Then a smile spread across his very wrinkled face. His eyes actually twinkled as he quickly translated Mac's question into the native Ininitka language.

There was huge laughter inside the hut—and Mac felt her face go red.

"You think *this* is our meal?" Mook asked her, still grinning broadly.

Mac gulped once. "Well, is it?" she asked again.

Mook laughed. "By the sea gods, no!" he said, throwing all the innards into some small pails nearby. "This is *garbage*. It's what we feed our dogs—and even they are not happy about it."

He picked up the bucket where the filets were being stored.

"This, my pale beauty, is our dinner," he said. "And a finer one you might never have."

Mac let out a long breath of relief and everyone in the hut laughed again.

Mac smiled, too.

"I'm sure you're right about that," she said.

The meal was delicious—as delicious as boiled herring filet could be.

The best thing about the fish was that there was plenty of it. The herring was naturally sweet and without bones to worry about—they'd been cooked away in the process—it all went down very easily.

Mac didn't realize how hungry she was until she started digging into her first plateful. After about a dozen bites, however, she glanced up to find that the entire hut was looking at her. She'd been eating with her hands—again simply because she assumed that that was the tradition. But when she looked up she saw that everyone else was eating with a knife and fork, thank you.

Again her face turned red as Mook handed some utensils to her. Again the place erupted in laughter—Mac's included.

Once the food had been dispensed with, Mook's nephews poured everyone a huge cup of a clear pinkish liquid. Mook assured Mac that the drink would cure "anything that is ailing you and a few things that aren't."

Mac had no idea what this after-dinner drink was made from. And after the two faux-pas, she was not going to ask. It definitely tasted fruity and sweet. And after a while she realized that, although not alcoholic, the drink was very soothing.

Mac had consumed about a half a cup when she noticed the colors in the hut seemed to be getting a bit brighter. The dull red paint of the ceiling, for example, suddenly seemed more vivid. The yellow of the bowls began glowing, the blue of the huge stew pot turned almost neon. Even the fire in the lanterns seemed different. Everything became warmer, glistening. Alive, almost.

Mac took a long, deep breath, and imagined she could see the warm air go in her mouth as a shade of blue, and come out as a shade of turquoise. She looked up at Mook and saw that he was smiling again. And she smiled, too.

"It is time for our story of the evening," Mook announced.

Those in attendance gathered closer around him. Men, women, children, old folk—all had consumed a cup of the pink juice. All were now waiting anxiously for what Mook had to say, Mac included.

"For the benefit of our guest," Mook began, "I will tell the story in her tongue."

Everyone in attendance nodded eagerly; a few actually patted Mac on the head.

"If you cannot understand a word, stop me and I'll translate for you," Mook told them.

Again, his words were met with a chorus of agreeing smiles and nods.

Mook doused several of the oil lanterns. Those that remained played sensuous shadows on the walls of the hut. Mac's head began to spin in the most pleasant way. She'd never felt quite like this before.

"Years ago," Mook began, his voice now a whisper, "our ancestors hunted not just whales and seals out in the deep sea. They hunted another creature—one much larger than a whale—that used to live off our shore.

"This creature had a very long neck and a body like that of a huge animal that walks the lands near the bot-

125

tom of the world. It had large flippers and a very long tail.

"This creature was so big, in fact, it could eat more fish in one gulp than our entire village could catch in one day."

This made the children in the room gasp. The adults shook their heads in amazement.

"This monstrous creature would swim in the waters fifty miles out. The ocean was so deep out there, and the winds so high, our hunters risked their lives just in hopes of seeing one of the monsters. They would leave in the morning and disappear over the horizon and not be seen again until very late the next day. More often than not, they would come back without ever coming across one of the big creatures."

Again the kids let out a chorus of amazed gasps.

"But every once in a while, our ancestors would snag one of these beasts. They would beat him over the head and then drag him all the way back to shore. When this happened, the village would have enough meat to last for an entire winter!"

The entire crowd gasped now—Mac included.

"That's how big these monsters were," Mook went on. "The hide from their skins would keep our forebears warm. Their bones would be used for spears and eating utensils. Their flesh and muscles would be eaten for months. Nothing was wasted. Everything was used. These creatures were a gift from the gods to us. And we could never, ever abuse that right."

"No, never," several of the natives responded.

"But then, the ghost ships first came to our shores," Mook said after a dramatic pause. "And they began hunting these creatures—many hundreds of years ago. And our ancestors battled with the strange men on these ships—but it was no use. They were too strong for the

Ininitka. They hunted these beasts until only one was left. And there was a danger that this last creature would die—and that we, the Ininitka, would die along with it."

"So what happened?" Mac heard herself ask.

"We made a deal with the last of the creatures," Mook replied. "We promised to bring it to a safe place where it could swim and live without interference from the ghost ships. In return, the monster told us where we could fish for more herring than we ever could have imagined. In fact, the monster agreed to tell us of this sacred place where the fish jump right into our nets!"

"There is such a place?" Mac asked. "Really?"

Mook smiled. "Really . . ."

"So we agreed to help the monster," Mook went on. "And on that day, our bravest hunters went out to sea and the last monster followed them. They avoided the ghost ships and paddled for many, many days and nights and finally reached the place where the Scots live now. And then our men picked up the monster-fish and carried it over land for many miles and finally put it in a very deep, cold lake—and that's where it lives even today. And that's why we are able to catch so many fish here every day—because the great creature told us where to go where the fish would jump right into our nets."

There was utter silence in the hut. Every eye was on Mook. Mac's head was still spinning. She wasn't quite sure if she had followed the story right. Had Mook just claimed that his ancestors were taking credit for putting the monster in Loch Ness?

She didn't know. But then Mook continued.

"That is why our esteemed visitor is here with us today," he went on, nodding to Mac. "The ghost ships have returned. I saw one and our friends down at the bottom of the island seem to know about them, too.

That's where I was yesterday, when you all missed me so much.''

More nods, more sighs of relief that Mook was among them again.

''And now that the ghost ships are back, we have to do something about it. The fish are not jumping into our nets anymore. And it has not been like this since the white hairs came here fifty years ago, when I was just a boy.''

''What can we do, Mook?'' one man asked. ''With no fish, we will all die.''

Mook raised his hand and calmed the room.

''That's why our friend is here,'' he said. ''Tonight, she and I will go out onto the ice. And we will look for the ghost ship—and if we find it, we will combine our magic with the friends at the bottom of our island and together we will make sure the ghost ship goes away—and that the fish jump into our nets again.''

''But what if there is trouble?'' another of the adult males asked. ''The area around No-Seals Bay is haunted. What spirits will protect you?''

Mook smiled again. ''I am not worried,'' he said. ''If we get into trouble, I see two birds helping us out. One is a great specimen, with huge wings. The other—well, the other is smaller and I am more familiar with it these days.''

There was a sigh of relief in the hut.

''There might be trouble,'' Mook concluded. ''But if there is, we will prevail. This I promise you.''

The next thing Mac knew, she was standing up and looking at the crowd before her.

''I promise this, too,'' she heard herself say. ''Really.''

• • •

Two hours later, they were out on the ice of No Seals Bay.

The sun had long since disappeared, but the stars were extremely bright, and the iridescent glow of the surrounding snow and ice combined to produce a different kind of light. Bluish, almost warm.

Mac was simply awestruck.

She was riding on one of the Ininitkas' motorized fishing boats. It was a twenty-two-foot vessel with a small winch, a small fish hold, a tiny wheelhouse, and not much else. It was so small, it looked like a miniature tugboat, something from a kid's imagination.

In front of her were six kayaks. They were leading the way, slowly, through the sunken ice field. No Seals Bay was actually a lake that Mac estimated was about one mile around. It was bordered on three sides by skyscraper-sized glacial cliffs. Each one was sheer, forbidding, and beautiful.

The fourth side of the bay was an outlet to the sea. It was here that the Ininitkas usually came, not to fish—because no fish or seals ever seemed to enter this place—but rather to try out new kayaks, or to teach the younger men of the village how to paddle, how to fix a kayak at sea, and how to get the feel of a newly constructed boat.

It was a strange place indeed. The water depth here looked deceptively shallow. Mac estimated that the draft was about twenty feet. But the reason why it was so strange was that below the field of ice, which Mook said he thought was about ten feet thick, were the real waters of the bay. And they ran very cold and very deep.

The fact that this was such an odd place, that it was here that Mook's nephew Week-wa had seen the dreaded lights under the ice, and that Mook himself had seen the "ghost ship" was not lost on Mac on this cold, almost surreal night. Mook and his five cousins were manning the kayaks in front of her. They were paddling very slowly in unison and each time their paddles would dip into the water they let out a noise that was a cross between a grunt and a yelp. After a while, Mac found the sound—like everything else around her—hypnotic.

The pink juice was still coursing its way through her veins, she assumed—and she wondered whether that had something to do with the absolutely majestic vibes she was feeling inside. The deep cold itself was beautiful. The stars, so incredibly bright. The chant each time six paddles hit the icy water. Mac had never experienced anything like this before. She doubted she ever would again.

But there was also a job she was supposed to be doing here and whenever she found her mind wandering and looking at all the beauty around her, she had to drag herself back to the matter at hand. After all, she was out here looking for the *Sea Shadow II*—possibly the most secret vessel the navy had ever built.

The question was, what would she do if and when they actually found it?

And would it really have a connection to the two murders out on the snow?

They drifted along the glassy water like this for two hours. If anything, the scenery got more beautiful, the surroundings more silent.

Mac estimated the time was now five minutes to midnight. The stars overhead were absolutely shimmering. . . .

"Freeka-doka!"

The blood-curdling cry carried across the bay and echoed back again several times. It was chilling.

Mac ran to the bow of the fishing boat and looked out onto the water. The six kayaks were right in front of her and glowing in the middle of them, deep below the submerged layer of ice, was an extremely bright yellow light.

The six men in the kayaks began screaming and paddling in all directions—anything to get away from the lights under the ice.

"My eyes!" someone yelled in the night. "They are falling out!"

"Don't look down!" Mac heard Mook screaming to them, but his warnings didn't do any good. The men in the kayaks continued madly paddling away.

The men steering the fishing boat began to panic as well. They gunned their engine, intent on leaving the area just as quickly as the kayakers—if not faster.

"Don't look down!" the skipper of the skiff was yelling at Mac now.

But Mac did not heed his warning. She *had* to look down—but not because of any mesmerizing effect of the lights. No, she was looking down because she knew exactly what this thing under the ice was.

"Stop!" she yelled up at the man behind the controls of the fishing boat. "Stay right here. We are not in any danger."

The man gunned the engine again—but then he threw it back into idle.

Mac brought out her flashlight and directed its beam down to where the lights were shining. The kayakers had dispersed, they were still screaming—all but Mook, that is. He had turned around and his kayak was now about fifty feet off the port side of the fishing boat.

"I know what this is!" Mac yelled again, watching as the lights under the ice began following the beam of her flashlight. "It is not an evil spirit. It is not here to hurt us. It is here to help us."

"Help us?" she heard Mook ask from the darkness.

Mac moved her flashlight's beam a bit closer to the bow of the fishing boat. The lights beneath the ice moved accordingly.

"See?" she called out. "It is doing what I tell it to. It moves when I move. Would your evil spirits do that?"

The skipper of the fishing boat was now standing beside her; so were the two other members of the crew. Sure enough, they saw that whenever Mac moved her flashlight beam, the glowing yellow light beneath the ice would move toward it.

"How?" the skipper gasped. "Your light—it has more magic than *freeka-doka*?"

"Nope," Mac replied, moving her beam off to starboard now. "That is not a god below us. It is a robot."

Actually, it was called a Remotely Piloted Submersible, or RIPS for short.

It was a new device the navy used to locate objects deep underwater, be they errant torpedoes, wayward weapons, or crashed airliners. RIPS could go out on a tether sometimes three to four miles long. It was usually controlled by someone on a so-called transfer ship. Mac knew one of the sensors on the RIPS was very sensitive to light. By moving her flashlight beam around, she knew the RIPS would probably move with it, sending signals back to its operator that it had picked up something unusual on its light-detection sensors.

In fact, Mac was sure that at that moment, the robot's operator was trying to position the RIPS to get its TV cameras looking up at her. If that happened, she planned to flash the TV camera a peace sign.

But even though she had solved this one mystery, it really didn't answer any questions other than that this was not the dreaded *freeka-doka* shining from below.

Indeed, the presence of the RIPS only confirmed that

the navy was up here looking for something . . . but what? There was even a chance, she suspected, that the RIPS was actually tethered to the *Sea Shadow II*—that would make the most sense, given that Mook ran into the stealth ship right here in No Seals Bay.

But again, knowing this did not fill in any blanks for Mac.

It only raised up new questions.

By this time, five of the six kayakers had paddled back in close to the fishing boat.

They seemed calmed by the fact that Mac was "controlling" the lights under the ice. Mook paddled right up to the side of the fishing boat and she hurriedly told him what RIPS was all about. He seemed to understand the concept of a robot under the water.

"There really isn't anything to fear," Mac told Mook. "It's just one of our government's things, intruding on your space."

Mook actually laughed. "It is not the first time," he said, his voice showing some relief as the RIPS gave up on Mac's light beam and started quickly moving away. "I just don't understand why other people want to come up here and bother us all the time. We are as far away from the rest of the world as you can get—you would think people would want to leave us alone."

It was only the fact that Mook was laughing when he said this that prevented Mac from feeling totally chauvinistic. The native Ininitka was right, of course. If there was anyone in this world who deserved to be left alone, it was the native people of Immaluost Island.

Mook had a whistle with him and with one long blow called the other kayakers to him. They all returned but one.

"Where is Saka?" Mook asked the others.

The others explained that when the lights had appeared under the ice, Saka had paddled faster than all of them to get away.

Now Mac moved her flashlight beam all around the bay—the searchlight on the fishing boat did this as well. And just by sheer luck, they saw the dim figure of Saka still paddling madly, rounding the southern edge of No Seals Bay and passing out of sight.

"We must get him," Mook said. "He'll get lost in the dark."

The remaining kayakers quickly boarded the fishing boat, and the skipper gave his vessel full power. Within five minutes, they were heading out of No Seals Bay at top speed, nose pointing south.

Mac had her radio out and was powering it up. She wanted to report her discovery of the RIPS robot in No Seals Bay to Harm.

Let him figure out what it means, she thought.

It took five more minutes for the small fishing boat to reach the southern end of No Seals Bay. The boat's motors were so loud, conversation between them was nearly impossible.

Only by yelling directly into Mac's ear could Mook tell her that Saka was the most inexperienced kayakers of the village adults. That's why he now feared for his well-being.

Mac reassured Mook that they would soon catch up with the wayward kayaker and take him aboard.

They rounded the point and now Mac saw that on the other side of the mountain was an even larger bay, this one very dark but practically free of ice. Off in the distance, she could see a dull glow of bluish lights.

"That is your place," Mook said. "The place your people jokingly call 'I'm Lost.'"

Mac studied the glow and figured that Immaluost Station was probably five miles down the rugged coastline—maybe three as the crow flies.

That would make this place very close to—

Her thoughts were interrupted when one of the crewmen suddenly gave a shout.

"Saka! There he is!"

Mac turned her flashlight in the direction the others were pointing and sure enough, there was Saka, bent over in his kayak, obviously exhausted from his mad dash away from No Seals Bay.

Mook let out a great sigh of relief.

"He is the only orphan in our village," the shaman said. "Everyone would have been very upset if something happened to him."

The skipper pulled alongside the kayak—and that's when Mac noticed something strange. Saka did not have his paddle with him. Had he dropped it? Two of the others climbed down the access ladder and pulled the wayward kayak closer to the fishing boat.

One man patted Saka on the back—but there was no response.

"Saka!" the boat's skipper yelled.

Nothing.

The man closest to him grabbed the collar of Saka's hood and pulled his head up. Saka flopped backwards and his face was now straight up, nose to the stars.

One of the men let out a long scream. There was blood everywhere. Horrified, Mac shone her flashlight down on the kayak. There was a gaping hole in Saka's chest, and another one near his right shoulder. But then she moved her light to the man's face and made an even more startling discovery.

Saka's eyeballs were missing.

• • •

Harm was sitting in the "Russian culture room" when the frantic call from Mac came in.

He'd just finished interviewing the thirty-one Russian "suspects" and had proven beyond all doubt that not one of them could have been involved in the murders.

Instead, the Russians were all admitting to being accomplices to the crimes simply because they saw it as a ticket out of I'm Lost Station. It was a good example of just how much some people hated the place. They would risk a murder trial and possible conviction just to go home.

It was really an embarrassing display, and most humiliating for the ex-KGB man, who had obviously been misinformed when his underlings first reported that they'd nabbed their suspects.

But none of this was bothering Harm at the moment. All that he was concerned about now was the note just handed to him by the station's communications officer.

A transmission had been picked up from Mac's radio. In the communication officer's words, she was "frantic."

The problem was, Harm had to run the length of the station to get to the radio room. This took him nearly seven minutes to do, even though he was running full out.

By the time he got there, the transmission had been lost.

However, a radioman had been smart enough to start a tape recorder and thus was able to get most of Mac's message.

It was indeed frantic.

The tape started off with a scream of static as Mac tried desperately to zero in on the best reception. Meanwhile, the radioman was telling her simply to talk louder.

Mac was trying hard to remain calm—Harm could tell by her voice. But something was wrong, wherever she was.

Very wrong.

Once the static cleared up, Mac began the message by attempting to tell her position. But she could do this only by describing the terrain around her. She said she could see the lights from Immaluost Station off in the distance, anywhere from five to seven miles to the south. She described the huge bay they were in as having high snow walls on three sides, with a wide entrance to the sea. The problem was, this description fit virtually every inlet on the island.

But then she started reporting that one of Mook's men had been shot with a high-caliber rifle. Twice in the head, twice in the upper body.

Then came the sound of a huge crash—there was no way to tell exactly what caused it.

There was a lot of confusion, then Mac yelled: "Harm, if you can hear this—or if anyone can—we are . . . we are looking at . . . I just don't believe this . . . I just don't believe it . . .".

And that's where the message ended.

eighteen ✈

THE DECK OFFICER OF THE DANISH PATROL
ship *Thyregod* was a lieutenant named Knusten Orbe.

Like almost everyone else on the ship, he disliked
coming to Immaluost Island except for one thing: the
American food in the mess hall. He loved American-
made hamburgers just as much as anyone, and he ate
his fill whenever possible. But other than that, a trip up
to Immaluost was usually a long, cold, arduous, dangerous affair. And even worse, once you arrived, nothing
ever happened up here.

Until now.

It was funny to see a grown man trying to run while
wearing the massively thick arctic outerwear that everyone at the station had to climb into if they had any
chance of surviving the forty-below temperatures on Immaluost Island.

It was even funnier to see three men running, dressed
this way. The amount of slipping, sliding, falling, rolling, and clawing back to one's feet only to fall again—it
was comical to watch even for a stoic Dane like Lieutenant Orbe.

This was what he was watching now. Three men in
heavy gear running—or trying to—through the station's

center field, up onto the walkway, over to the main dock area, and out onto the stone-and-wood pier itself.

At first Orbe was convinced the three men were Russians. The warship *Zirovalksk* was tied up two berths over from his ship, and Orbe was certain that these three buffoons were three drunk Russians, racing each other back to their vessel, most probably for the prize of yet another bottle of vodka.

But when the trio ran right past the *Zirovalksk*, Orbe, watching all this from the heated bridge of his vessel, began to take even more notice. The next ship in line was the U.S. Coast Guard icebreaker *Polar Star*.

Americans? Drunk? And trying to get back to their ship? No, that didn't seem to fit. If anything, Orbe knew the Americans here could be even more boring and granitelike than his own countrymen.

So when the three dark figures raced past the gangway for the *Polar Star*, Orbe got up out of his seat and pressed his face against the frosted bridge window. The three men, still slipping and sliding, had reached the pier right next to his ship. Orbe watched, startled now, as the trio stopped at the bottom of the *Thyregod*'s gangway for a few seconds, had a hasty discussion, and then began charging up the walkway.

My god, Orbe thought. *They're coming here?*

Yes, they were. In fact, in less than ten seconds, they were banging at the bridge door.

Orbe calmly called down to the captain's quarters and informed him that there were ''likely unauthorized personnel'' on the ship. But by that time the banging on the bridge door had become so loud, Orbe had no choice but to open it. The three men tumbled in.

Orbe took a look at them and decided he'd been only one-third correct when he'd first assumed the three men were drunken Russians. As it turned out, there was only one Russian. The other two men were Americans.

And they didn't seem drunk at all.

One came right up to Orbe's face. This man was a handsome, very sober American officer. He was breathing mightily from his long sprint here. His eyes were on fire.

"Do you speak English?" he was asking Orbe.

"I do," Orbe replied. "What is the matter here?"

"This ship," the American was saying. "Does it have a helicopter? One that can carry at least five people?"

Orbe just stared back at them.

"You're here to inquire about our helicopter?"

A smile came across the American's face. Not one of joy, but one of relief. That's when Orbe realized for the first time that these men were carrying weapons.

"We're not here just to inquire about it," Harm told him. "We're here to borrow it."

The Danish ship *Thyregod* was actually a small frigate adapted for polar patrol duty. Like the *Polar Star*, it carried a helicopter. But unlike the American icebreaker, the Danish helo was originally designed for combat.

It was a Westland Lynx Model E. It was a rugged aircraft, capable of carrying antiship missiles, torpedoes, heavy machine guns, and cannons. But at the moment, its best feature was that it could carry up to a half-dozen people and move them very quickly.

It took but a few minutes of "negotiations" between Thorpe—who was the second American in the trio of slipping heavily clad men who had invaded the *Thyregod*—and the captain of the Danish ship, to get use of the Danes' Westland helo.

Mac was in trouble—big trouble—and the quickest way Harm could think of getting to her was by helicopter. The *Polar Star*'s Dolphin helo was much too small for this emergency mission. The Russian ships carried no helicopters. That left it up to the Danes to come to the rescue.

But they had one condition. The Danish captain insisted that one of his officers pilot the aircraft. This made for a very unusual crew climbing aboard the hot-started Lynx: Harm, Thorpe, a Russian naval officer named Crekov whom Thorpe suggested they bring along for purely political reasons, and the Danish pilot, who turned out to be the rather hapless Lieutenant Orbe.

One of the features of the Lynx was that it could be hauled out of its storage shed, engines started, controls turned on and brought up to snuff and ready for lift off all within ten minutes' time. But even this was too long for Harm. He was sitting nervously in the copilot's right-hand seat, urging the others to get aboard and get strapped in, and urging the pilot to take off even before all his oil-pressure gauges read safe. Urging him to *go . . . go . . . go!*

Finally the helo lifted off, its engines screaming madly in the sub-zero temperatures. Harm's instruction to Orbe—who indeed understood English very well— was simply to follow the coastline up from the research station until they saw anything unusual. But in the back of his mind, Harm had the feeling he knew exactly where Mac was. That's why he told the helicopter pilot to proceed without turning on the aircraft's powerful search lantern.

The Lynx went up cleanly, its nose dipping forward a bit. It hovered for a moment and then off it went in a rush of power and exhaust. With its engines in full roar, it passed directly over the research facility and disappeared into the night.

• • •

It was a strange dream that Bud Roberts had during his nearly eighteen hours of uninterrupted sleep in the ice station's mess hall.

He was back in Thule, playing in the big golf tournament. He was in a foursome with an admiral, an army general, and a nun. His group was the last to tee off. As they were hitting, they received word that the winning score was ninety-nine. It was said to be unbeatable.

Bud had come up with a secret weapon, however. Earlier in the dream, he had observed other players stacking their bright orange golf balls in the shape of huge pyramids inside the Thule officers' club. He had asked someone why the other players had done this. Bud had been told by a man dressed like a hockey player that it was to raise the temperature of the inner core of the ball.

Even in his dream, Bud had to question this peculiar notion of physics. Raising the temperature of the inner core of the golf ball would not necessarily aid in furthering its flight once it was out in the extremely frigid environment. Flashing back to a high school science class, he seemed to recall someone telling him that it is easier to make something cold than to make it hot—or was that the other way around? In any case, in this jumbled-up dream, spurred on no doubt by high ingestion of chocolate milk followed by a forbidden cup of coffee, Bud had come up with an alternative.

So before he teed off, he had all his golf balls set out in the snow. And when he finally hit his first drive—well, the ball went a mile and a half.

And that's when astronaut Alan Shepard came down out of the clouds and shook his hand.

And that's when Bud heard an ear-splitting scream and looked up to see a huge black bird passing over his head.

And that's when he finally woke up.

• • •

He didn't know where he was at first.

When his eyes finally opened, they presented him with a sideways view of the mess hall, now all but empty. He lifted his head slightly from the sticky cafeteria table, and sleepily moved his jaw back and forth. The feeling in it started to return.

He yawned once and fought the idea of returning to sleep. That's when the mess hall began shaking for real and a sound like the one in his dream invaded his ears again. He looked outside to see the Danish navy's helicopter fly right over the mess hall and vanish over the hills to the north.

That was enough to wake Bud fully. Now he sat straight up, feeling no less self-conscious than a hangover reveler waking up on a park bench somewhere. He once again scanned the mess through hazy eyes and saw that all of the tables around him were thankfully empty. Bud let out a short sigh of relief. While he was sure many people had come and gone while he had slept, at least no one would see him wake up and make his escape.

But then he looked to his right and that's when he realized that not only was he not alone in the mess, but there was a man sitting right across the table from him.

Bud tried to sit up even straighter—perhaps he could fool this guy into thinking that he'd only been here a few minutes. But he could tell the other man was not buying that. In fact, the man couldn't have cared less. He was just sitting there, idly sipping his coffee, pulling slightly on his pure white goatee. Bud finally recognized him. It was Dr. Heidkamp, the senior scientist at the Immaluost facility.

"You speak Ukrainian, I see," he said to Bud casually. "Or are you just doodling?"

For a moment, Bud thought he was back in his dream.

"Excuse me, sir? What did you say?"

Heidkamp pointed to the scrap of paper in front of Bud's napkin/pillow.

"Those words," he said. "They are Ukrainian. Many people confuse them with being Russian."

Bud looked at his scribbled sheet. *Ukrainian?*

Heidkamp smiled and sipped his coffee. "I've been waiting for you to wake up, just to tell you that," he said in his odd singsongy voice. "You'd best not show any inclination toward the Ukrainian way of life up here though, my boy. There are too many Russians about. They are two peoples that just don't get along."

Finally coming out of his haze, things began making some sense for Bud.

He pulled the shell casing from his pocket and showed it to Heidkamp.

"These words, sir," he said. "Can you read them? Can you identify them as being Ukrainian?"

Heidkamp took the shell, adjusted his glasses on the tip of his nose in the manner that all superior-thinking academics seemed to do, and studied the casing.

"Yes," he said after a few moments. "I would definitely say this is Ukrainian and that this is actually some kind of military stamp on the bottom. May I ask where you got it? A souvenir of some sort?"

Luckily Bud was thinking more clearly now.

"Yes, that's it exactly," he said, biting his lip. His mind was racing now, an inevitable rush of thoughts and notions that his brain needed in order to make up for its eighteen idle hours.

"May I ask you another question, sir?"

Heidkamp's eyes lit up. He loved it when people came to him for his opinion. Even if it had nothing to do with ice.

"Certainly, my son," he replied with a wide smile. "Ask away."

Bud looked him straight in the eye. "Do you know what the term 'clean steel' means?"

nineteen ✈

ONE OF THE BEST FEATURES OF THE WEST-
land Lynx was that as far as helicopters went, it was a
relatively quiet machine.

It had to do with the engines' sound dampers, muf-
flers, and the fact that the power plants actually got qui-
eter once the aircraft was up and flying.

As it turned out, the flight in the Danish helo was a
brief one. Going purely on instinct, Harm had Lieutenant
Orbe fly up to the place he knew as Lookout Point, the
site of the murders. Orbe killed all of his exterior lights
and set the helo down on the field of snow where the
bodies had been found, using the orange and yellow tape
markers to guide himself in.

He killed the Lynx's engine as soon as its skids hit
the ice. In a matter of seconds there was nothing but the
wind and the whirring as the helo's rotors quickly
wound down. No one inside the helo said anything for
at least a minute. Finally the rotor stopped turning and
then there was only the wind.

"I hope your gut instinct is right," Thorpe finally
whispered to Harm, breaking the silence.

Harm did not reply. All that he could think of at the
moment was the last time he'd seen Mac, lifting away

in the Dolphin helo, waving good-bye. The thought that had gone through his mind at that moment was that he'd never see her again. Would that sad intuition somehow come true?

The Danish pilot opened up his door and indicated that Harm should do the same. As quietly as they could, the four men got out and lowered themselves to the crunchy snow below. The wind was picking up and the temperature suddenly felt even colder than before—if a drop from thirty below zero to thirty-five below could actually be detected.

The four of them stood there for a moment. They were all carrying weapons. Harm and Thorpe had M-16s especially adapted for the polar environment. The Russian had an AK-47 covered in fur. The Dane was carrying a Glock machine-pistol. Of them all, it was Orbe the Dane who was the most baffled. All he knew was that they were looking for Harm's colleague—a woman who somehow had found herself way up here in the middle of nowhere and had yet managed to find some danger to fall into.

"Okay, it's your show, Harm," Thorpe told him, looking around nervously. "Though I don't mind telling you this place gives me the creeps every time I come up here."

"That's something that must be catching," Harm replied.

He took a long look around and let out a breath of very cold air. Why had he come here? Certainly Mac had not been on land when she'd made her desperate call. So why here?

Harm wasn't really sure—but something deep inside him was saying *this* was the place to be. *This* was the place to begin the search for Mac.

For a moment, he even thought he could hear his father's voice whispering in his ear. *Look around, son. What's different here? What does not fit? What doesn't seem right?*

Harm turned a full 360 degrees. What didn't seem right here?

Suddenly he stopped. He was facing the ridge that led to the top of the cliff from which the place got its name. He squinted—was that a faint glow of light over the rise?

He pushed the fur from his hood away from his eyes and looked again. Yes—there *was* a greenish glow— faint, barely detectable, coming from right over the top of the rise.

"There!" Harm called out to the others. "Let's start by looking up there!"

The three others just looked at him and shrugged.

"It's your party, Harm," Thorpe told him.

With that, all four men started the difficult climb up the short rise. There had been a fierce storm in the area since the last time Harm had been here, and now just about everything had a thick coating of ice on it—the rise included. Even worse, the wind took this very inopportune time to start gusting, and the small team had to stop several times and let the worst of the gale pass by.

When they reached the steepest part of the climb, they had to resort to a hand-over-hand climbing system. Harm would go up several feet, dig the tips of his boots into the ice-caked snow, then reach down and pull Thorpe up and past him. The process was then repeated as the Russian came up next. Then came the Dane. Then, by using their backs and shoulders, Harm was able to pull himself up over the three of them, reaching the half-way point. Then the process was repeated all over again.

By the third time they accomplished this, Harm had

come within ten feet of the top. Thorpe then crawled up the human ladder and with one great lunge, finally gained the top of the icy ridge. Exhausted, he lay there for a moment, catching his breath and then trying to orient himself.

Then he looked off to the northeast and let out a gasp that could be heard over the strongest of gales.

"God . . ." he said. *"I don't believe this!"*

Despite the cold, Harm's ears started to burn. Those were the same words he'd last heard from Mac.

"What is it?" he screamed up at Thorpe, but there was no way the officer was going to answer him. Whatever was happening on the other side of the ridge had knocked him speechless.

The Russian came scrambling over Harm's back next, and with help from Thorpe, got himself dragged to the top as well.

Thorpe pointed to something and the Russian let out an almost identical gasp. He started spewing something in Russian; Harm did not need to speak the language to know it translated into: *I don't believe this!*

The Dane was climbing up Harm's back now and he, too, was hauled to the top of the ridge. He took one look toward the north—and tried to climb back down the hill again! He stayed put only because Thorpe and the Russian grabbed him.

"What the hell is going on?" Harm yelled up at them.

But instead of answering his question, the three men simply reached down and roughly hauled him up to the top of the ridge.

As soon as Harm gained the top, however, Thorpe pushed his face into the snow. A second later, a searchlight swept right over them.

Thorpe finally let him up, and Harm pushed some of the ice and snow from his face. His whole body was shaking now; it was like he was hooked up to an electrical generator—or better yet, like he'd been zapped by a bolt of lightning. What had the other three seen that had affected them so?

He was about to find out.

Harm wiped the last of the ice from his eyes and found himself lying flat next to Thorpe.

"What the hell is it?" he demanded of the navy officer.

Thorpe's gaze never wavered.

"Do you believe in ghosts, Harm?" he asked him, his voice sounding like he was in a hypnotic spell.

"What?" was Harm's only reply.

"Take a look," Thorpe urged him.

And finally Harm did so—and a second later, he saw what they had seen and he, too, felt like he had suddenly gone mad.

"This is crazy," Harm heard himself say. "This can't be happening . . ."

But it was. On the other side of the hill, the old German replenishment station—the rotten wooded house he'd seen less than two days before—was now alive with lights burning, inside and out. And men in dark outerwear with searchlights and weapons were moving all around it.

But this was not what had put the fear of God in them all.

No, it was what was sitting about five hundred feet offshore.

Anchored there, nearly hidden in a swirl of icy fog, was a German U-boat.

twenty ✈

IT SEEMED IMPOSSIBLE, BUT JUST THIRTY minutes after waking up from an eighteen-hour nap, Bud Roberts was ready to go back to sleep again.

He was sitting in the very prim office of Dr. Heidkamp, his eyes getting heavy, feet getting pins and needles from inactivity, listening but not hearing the scientist drone on and on and on—about ice.

"There would be no life on earth if it hadn't been for ice," Heidkamp was saying for what Bud was sure had to be the twentieth time in the past half-hour. "From ice came water, from water came life. I am, among admittedly few of my peers, convinced that the secret of life itself will someday be found in ice. Whether it is here at the North Pole, or at the exact opposite end of the globe, where, we all know there has been . . ."

More than once in the last tortuous half-hour, the thought went through Bud's mind that Heidkamp was so pompous and boring, living in the North Pole was actually too good for him.

There was an internal battle raging inside Bud's head

153

now. He, too, had learned patience during his tenure at JAG. It was the key to just about everything—both Harm and Admiral Chegwidden had taught him that.

But at what point did politeness have to take a back-seat to expediency? Heidkamp claimed he knew the meaning of 'clean steel.' The question was, how long did Bud have to endure a nonstop lecture on the aspects of frozen water before he could politely break in and ask the doctor to shut up and get to the point at hand?

"Now, of course, we know there is ice in outer space," Heidkamp was saying. "And, I'm sure, that once we fly out to the stars, we will find just as much, if not—"

"Excuse me, sir," Bud suddenly heard himself interrupting. He was surprised at the sound of his own voice.

Heidkamp was, too.

"Yes, young man?" he asked. "What is it?"

"I don't give a *damn* about ice, sir . . . ," Bud heard the words come out of his mouth.

"Excuse me?"

"No one does, sir," Bud replied, panic rising up inside of him. Where was this coming from? "No one cares about ice, and at the moment, I especially don't, sir. . . ."

Heidkamp just stared back at him, his mouth open a little, studying Bud through his trifocals. It was quite possible that in his thirty-five-year academic career, no one had ever talked to him quite like this. He was momentarily stumped for a reply.

"Well," he said finally. "What *are* you interested in, son?"

Bud took the deepest breath of his life.

"Cold steel, sir," he said with some vigor. "That's why I came here in the first place."

Heidkamp just continued staring back at him.

"Don't you remember, sir?"

It was weird what happened next. It was as if someone had turned off one switch inside Heidkamp's overfilled brain and flipped another one on. He took a breath, closed his eyes, opened them, and smiled.

"Clean steel?" he said. "Sure, I know all about that, too."

"Please, sir," Bud said, leaning forward. "Please tell me."

Heidkamp sat back in his chair, removed his glasses, and folded his arms across his chest.

"Simply put," he began, ironically enough, "clean steel is steel manufactured without contamination from unnatural atomic radiation. Beginning in 1945 with the first atomic bomb test at Los Alamos, through the bombings of Hiroshima and Nagasaki and during all the atomic testing of the 1950s, every piece of steel manufactured is contaminated with microscopic amounts of radiation—stuff that is just floating around us every day. Now, even though these amounts are, in most cases, minuscule, they are large enough to throw very sensitive equipment off-kilter, should they be made of anything but clean steel."

"What kind of sensitive equipment, sir?" Bud asked, literally on the edge of his seat.

"Well, these days, you name it, son," Heidkamp replied. "Clean steel is particularly important in the manufacture of satellites, precision medical instruments. Missile guidance systems. Nuclear warheads."

Nuclear warheads? Bud didn't like the sound of that.

"But sir, surely not every piece of steel these days is contaminated," Bud said. "Or is it?"

"Well, your question is a bit moot," Heidkamp replied. "You see, U.S. scientists eventually discovered a process to make clean steel in a factory. But before they came up with this process—and in the years immediately following the dawn of the Atomic Age—clean steel was essential to making A-bombs, among other things. So the government obtained all its clean steel from the wrecks of sunken World War Two ships, especially those that went down in extremely cold waters.''

Heidkamp actually laughed a little bit.

"As it turns out," he went on, "the largest source of such vessels were German U-boats sunk in the North Sea, mostly in the area between Iceland and Scotland, but all throughout the Arctic as well.''

"Wow . . . ," was all Bud could say.

"Now, of course, while the United States and its closest allies know how to manufacture their own clean steel, I'm sure there are some unsavory types around the world today that would pay a lot of money to get their hands on some. And because the United States would not export any of this technology to anyone of nefarious means, I would think that going back to the original source of clean steel—that is, diving and salvaging steel from old wrecks, would probably be the only other way to get hold of such a valuable commodity. I would even venture to guess that anyone in need of clean steel might pay its worth in gold, or even more.

"So you see, any wrecks still at the bottom of the cold waters up here would be very valuable. And of course that's where ice comes into this. Because it is the water up here that is, in fact, in a prefrozen condition that allows for . . .''

It was at this point that Dr. Heidkamp looked up and realized he was talking to himself—again.

Bud Roberts was long gone.

• • •

Commander McKinney was just drifting off to sleep when Bud burst into his cabin.

McKinney was sitting behind his desk, head back, tie loosened, feet up and resting on an open drawer. Slumped in one chair was Dr. Spokosvitch; next to her was Dr. Oblomov. Both were still hiding inside McKinney's cabin, still not wanting to have anything to do with the Russian military men who had taken over half of Immaluost Station.

Both of the Russian scientists woke up at Bud's sudden entrance. The lights in the cabin were on—and Bud wound up staring at the two elderly scientists for a few very awkward seconds.

Why were they looking at him so queerly?

It was probably because Bud had made the sprint from the ice station across the dock to the pier, past the guards, and up the gangway—a trip of at least a hundred yards—dressed in nothing heavier than a sweatshirt, jeans, and sneakers.

It was so weird to see someone just in out of the cold, not wearing several layers of big, thick outerwear from head to toe.

McKinney took full measure of Bud as well—and asked the inevitable question.

"Are you inebriated, sailor?"

Bud was stopped cold by the ship commander's question.

"Absolutely not!" he gasped.

It was probably a breach of military etiquette not to have addressed McKinney as "sir" as well as failing to request proper permission to come aboard his ship. But for once Bud did not have time for such military niceties. He was in fear for Harm's and Mac's lives—he didn't really have time for anything else.

"Sir, do you know the whereabouts of Commander Rabb and Major Mackenzie?"

McKinney was a bit stumped by this. He'd been told that Harm and three others had gone off aboard the Danish ship's helicopter on some kind of "recon mission"—and he knew that Mackenzie had left for the native settlement the day before. But beyond that, he knew very little else.

"You don't know where your two superior officers are, Lieutenant?" McKinney asked Bud instead.

Bud finally took a long, deep breath. The ice was dripping off of him now, forming a small puddle beneath his feat.

"Sir, I think I'd better explain. . . ."

And explain he did. About the mysterious shell casing. About what he had heard down at Thule. About clean steel. McKinney knew some of this information already—but he didn't prevent Bud from spilling it all out.

At the end of his report, the two Russian scientists seemed as intrigued, if not more so, as McKinney.

Oblomov especially.

"Clean steel?" he said. "My God, I haven't heard that term in twenty years."

"I have to believe that what has been going on up here," Bud said, "everything, from these strange lights to the *Sea Shadow* to the murders, all must be connected somehow. It would be just too much of a coincidence if they all weren't."

McKinney and the two Russians considered this. Bud's logic appeared sound. There was just too much happening in this very isolated spot on the globe for it not to be all wrapped in one.

McKinney immediately punched his phone and got

his security officer on the line. He put the man on the speakerphone.

His query to the security officer man was simple: "Where is Commander Rabb at his moment?"

It took about thirty seconds to get a reply. "Still off the compound, sir."

"Do the Danes know where their helo is at this moment?"

Another thirty seconds.

"No, sir."

"Can they get a reading? A radar indication, or a radio fix?"

Another thirty.

"They are trying, sir."

"In my opinion, if there is any country that is looking for clean steel, it is the Ukraine," Dr. Spokosvitch said.

"I agree," Oblomov added. "They have been trying to develop their own guidance systems for years. Their own warheads, too. Despite these agreements they have with you westerners—there is a faction in Ukraine who want to be able to push a button and launch against Russia should that dark day come."

"There is also the possibility that they are manufacturing these things for sale to others," Spokosvitch said. "They are hard up for cash—and nothing sells so well on the black market as nuclear weapons technology."

Bud said, "It seems that with the shell casing and the events up near the crime scene—well sir, I just think maybe we should get up there—pronto!"

McKinney thought a moment and then stood up and tightened his tie.

"Lieutenant," he said. "I agree with you."

twenty-one ✈

LIEUTENANT COMMANDER HARMON RABB, U.S.
Navy, was killed in the line of duty near the Arctic Naval Research Station on Immaluost Island in the Greenland Sea. . . .

These words, and even more dire ones, had been running through Harm's mind for nearly thirty minutes
now. Was this how it was going to end? Really? In the
most isolated place on the planet? Stuck in three feet of
frozen snow, a bullet wound to the head or chest, or
maybe a mortal injury that would allow the life to just
leak out of him until the cold got him—or the polar
bears did. . . .

They say that in combat, in the moments before you
die, everything looks like it is happening in slow motion.
The real world suddenly shuts down and a surreal world
takes over. People talk to you, but you can't really hear
them. Bullets are whizzing by, and explosions are going
off all around you, but you cannot feel their effects—
not immediately, anyway. Everything that had been familiar to you changes.

When you are getting ready to pass from one place to
another, that slow-motion thing is the big clue . . .

The strange thing was, Harm seemed to have been

going in slow motion for the past half-hour. So many strange things had happened in that time—things that would seem almost impossible to jam into a mere eighteen hundred seconds—that his brain was close to a serious overload.

First of all, they were under attack—and had been for the last fifteen minutes. Before that, Harm has seen things that looked like they were out of a horror movie, a ghost movie, or a science-fiction movie.

It all started with the rather bizarre discovery that a U-boat was sitting at anchor in the bay below Lookout Point. As much as Harm's mind—sluggish and stalling due to the subzero weather—tried to tell him that what he was seeing wasn't really there, it was. He knew he wasn't totally crazy simply because the three other men with him saw it, too.

It was a large, thin, ancient-looking submarine. The German insignia on its conning tower was still clearly visible, as was the numbers on its side, which read U-237.

The sub was painted light gray with hundreds of black and dark-gray splotches dotting it; this was a "nautical disbursement" camouflage scheme not seen since the end of World War Two. The sub's deck gun was intact, as were its snorkel tubes and its periscope.

But just as this vessel was most certainly here, at anchor in the harbor, there were some odd things going on around it. There were several crews of black-suited men, some apparently wearing arctic-style deep-sea diving outfits, working on or around the vessel. Just below the waterline, several lengths of bright-orange bags could be seen. They were inflatables. The sub was also wrapped on its bow and stern in heavy cable, the lines of which ran deeper into the water. The sharp blue light from acetylene torches could also be seen up and down the length of the sub.

All of this told Harm and the others that what they had stumbled upon was not some ghostly event, but actually a salvage operation. These mysterious men below them—and there were at least three dozen of them on the beach alone—had somehow raised this submarine from the chilly depths and were now in the process of cutting it up.

And that's when another strange thing happened to Harm—one of many in this very long, very perilous night.

Harm did not easily accept the idea of a mystical world. He didn't really believe in ESP, psychic thought transfers, mind-reading, or anything of that nature. He wasn't sure why he didn't believe in this stuff, exactly—maybe to his mind, life was mysterious enough, without the fringe accoutrements.

But several minutes after they'd discovered the U-boat in Lookout Point Bay, and after it was obvious that the men in black were cutting it up, a very strange notion popped into his head.

Like a snatch from another person's dream, a voice whispered in his ear.

Clean steel . . .

And suddenly, he knew what it was.

He grabbed Thorpe's arm, and speaking faster than he'd ever done before, he gave him an almost textbook definition of clean steel: steel manufactured before the atomic explosions of the mid-forties, in which the ore grade is not contaminated by minute radioactive particles. Particularly useful in the manufacture of missile guidance systems, nuclear warheads, medical instruments, and satellite technology.

Thorpe just stared back at him.

"Where the hell did that come from?" he asked Harm.

Harm could only shrug. "I'm not really sure," was his only explanation.

But then Thorpe's brain kicked in, too, and *he* recalled hearing about the concept of clean steel. Even the Russian officer—hearing a piece of their conversation—chimed in with: "We invented the factory process of making clean steel in 1947 and your intelligence services stole it away from us."

Thorpe just looked over at the Russian and in as dry a voice as he could muster in this sub-zero gale, said, "Yeah whatever."

But now the idea that the clean steel concept was behind the mysteries on Immaluost Island began to make a lot of sense.

"Let's say the U.S. government gets wind that some unsavory foreign power that cannot manufacture clean steel on its own is snooping around the arctic depths, looking for the stuff the old-fashioned way," Harm said. "They locate a U-boat sunk around here nearly fifty years ago—and begin a salvage operation.

"The navy and the air force are sent up here to look into this situation. And to underscore how important they think it is, no less than a super secret stealth ship, some underwater robots, a wing of B-1 bombers and even the ultrasophisticated J-STARS aircraft are dispatched to the great frozen north. How's that for a theory?"

"But if that was so," Thorpe whispered back as they remained in place on the ridge looking down at the unreal events unfolding before them, "Howcome the navy and the air force, with all their doodads, never found these guys?"

It was a good question—one that was answered not ten seconds after Thorpe asked it.

It started out as a split-second flare of light coming from the entrance of Lookout Point Bay, perhaps two miles from the ridge where the four men were positioned. Harm looked straight up and saw the faint yellow-and-red streak rise and then start to fall. It was a weapon of some sort, fired by a vessel still hidden in the dark—and it was heading right for them.

Harm had no more time than to yell out "Get down!" when the ground beneath them was rocked by a huge explosion, the noise of which was so loud, Harm's ears felt like someone had suddenly stuck nails in them.

When he finally felt brave enough to raise his head, he saw that this weapon—most likely a precision-guided munition—had not been targeted at them. No, whoever had pulled the trigger on this one had a bigger target in mind. And to their chagrin, the aim had been perfect. For behind them the Danish Lynx helicopter was now nothing more than a hulk of twisted metal engulfed in a flame so intense, it was slowly creating a hole in the frozen ground beneath it, effectively burying the destroyed aircraft even as it burned. The Russian was simply frozen, looking at the burning wreckage; Orbe, the Danish officer, was close to tears.

"Damn," Thorpe breathed. "Where the hell did *that* come from?"

Again he got his answer a few seconds later when they saw another unusual vessel steam into the bay. It was by all appearances a typical fishing trawler, one that was outfitted for the harsh polar environment. But it was also clear that this vessel was sporting a number of weapons, including a ship-to-shore missile launcher, which its crew had just used to erase the Danish helo.

"I guess the navy and the air force weren't looking

for a fishing boat, exactly,'' Thorpe said. "These guys were probably under their noses all the time. It was the perfect disguise up here."

"They must have seen us land, and keyed into the helo's heat signature," Harm theorized correctly. "That missile shot was right on the money."

"And now they know we are up here and we ain't got no way to get out," Thorpe moaned, describing their situation in starkly accurate terms.

"I don't believe in God," the Russian Crekov was saying in thick English under his breath, "but I believe He can punish us. That's what's about to happen to us now."

This did seem to be the case. For after the missile vaporized the helo, a group of about a dozen men down on the beach began scanning the ridge with a searchlight again. Shortly after this, six of them could be seen picking up weapons and beginning to climb the cliff, three by way of a crude path cut out of its side on its northern face, the other three taking the longer, southern route.

Without a word, the four men laying flat on the ridge began checking their weapons' ammo clips.

"Not the best place for a gunfight," Thorpe was saying, making sure the clip in his M-16 was still unfrozen.

"I think they'd drop another missile on us if they didn't think it would cause too much of a commotion," Harm theorized grimly.

"More likely we are not worth another such missile," the Russian said.

"Bullets are cheaper," Orbe, the Dane said, his voice deep, as if now he truly had a reason to brood.

So now they had an armed gang coming up for them—and it flashed through Harm's mind that this was probably exactly what had happened to Sergei Bodachenko and Lieutenant Lapkin. They had stumbled onto the beginnings of this operation and those behind it had killed them in cold blood.

"And chopped them up to make it look like polar bears," Thorpe said, thinking the exact same thing as Harm, adding grimly, "At least we won't go to our graves with that question still open."

But at that moment, Harm wasn't really listening. He had spotted something else going on down below them, something that cut even deeper to his core than the discovery of the salvage operation and the destruction of their helicopter.

Down below on the beach, in front of the old German replenishment building, he saw that four gunmen were leading nine people out onto the rocky, icy shore. Harm put his binoculars to his eyes and jammed them up to full power.

Eight of the people were natives—there was no mistaking their dark skin and long hair.

The ninth person was Mac.

As the four men on the ridge watched in horror, the gunmen below separated one of the natives from the rest, stood him against the wall of the old building and shot him, point-blank in the chest.

"No!" someone screamed. Whether it came from the ridge or down below, there was no way of telling. The cry echoed mightily throughout the bay.

It did not stop the gunmen below, however. They simply picked up the dead native's body, threw it into the shallow water, and selected another man from the group.

That's when the sound of gunfire echoed throughout the bay again—but this time it was not coming from the cold-blooded killers on the beach. No—the gunfire was coming from Harm's M-16. He had suddenly found himself standing up and firing madly at the two gunmen just as they were about to execute the second native.

He knew in an instant that this was a very stupid thing for him to do—but he did not care. He would not stand by and watch innocent people get killed simply because they had been in the wrong place at the wrong time. And the fact that Mac was down there and might be next in line to be shot down . . . well, it was just too much for Harm to take. So he was emptying his clip in the general direction of the gunmen and this served both to scatter the remaining hostages and send the gunmen scurrying for cover as well.

The wild firing had served another purpose as well— one that was not good at all. It had exposed their position on the ridge and many men on the beach below began firing up at them.

That's when all hell broke loose. For as Harm was jamming another clip in his M-16—he had brought five in all—his partners on the ridge, quite bravely, opened up with their weapons as well.

Suddenly the frozen arctic night was afire with high-speed bullets, whizzing every which way—searing the snow in front of them, one catching the edge of Harm's parka, another ripping off part of Thorpe's boot.

And *that's* when everything went into slow motion.

And that's how it was right now. . . .

Thorpe jammed another clip into his rifle. The Russian was doing the same thing.

"I can't stay up here," Harm told them. "I've got to get to the beach. I've got to try and help Mac and those natives."

"That's a tall order for just one person, my friend," Thorpe told him. "So maybe Ivan will go with you. We'll stay up here and cover you."

"I will go," the Russian declared. "These people

killed one of my countrymen. I must try to right his death.''

Harm and Thorpe just looked at each other—again it was all in slow motion, as if the world itself had slowed on its axis, dragging time down along with it.

At that moment the chance that they would ever see each other alive again was very remote.

So they shook hands.

"Nice knowing you," Thorpe told Harm, his voice sounding like a vinyl record set to the slowest speed.

Somehow Harm remained upbeat. "When this is over, you owe me a beer," he said.

"Deal," Thorpe replied with a smile.

Harm then patted the Dane on the back and began crawling off to the right. The Russian was right on his heels.

Even though the world was suddenly going by in slow motion, Harm knew he had to make a quick decision here. There were bullets flying everywhere, the heavily armed fishing boat had moved further into the bay, and just about everyone on the beach was looking up and firing at the ridge.

The question was, how could he and the Russian get down to the beach, in short order, and somewhat stealthily, in time to do any good?

Harm really didn't know. The cliff before them dropped off at an almost seventy degree angle and it was thick with snow and thickly encrusted ice on its top. Trying to climb down would be impossible. And climbing down the outcrop of rocks sticking out at irregular places along the ridge would be just as foolhardy.

As it turned out, Crekov came up with the solution. It was simple, direct, crude, courageous. Typically Russian.

He simply put his feet over the edge of the cliff and

pushed himself off. In seconds he was sliding very fast down the side of the steep incline, his weapon up, firing wildly.

"Gawd!" Harm heard himself say, his words sounding oddly deep.

The next thing he knew, he too was sliding down the side of the hill, bullets pinging off the ice all around him, his feet throwing up great sprays of ice particles.

He landed hard and in a heap in the exact same spot where the Russian had arrived just seconds earlier. It was a miracle they didn't shoot each other in the process of getting disentangled from one another. But somehow they managed to get to the shelter of some beach rocks.

The Russian never stopped firing—and neither did the men on the beach. The air was filled with streaks of tracer fire coming from the gunmen. Harm and the Russian were only about fifty yards from the replenishment building now, and they could still see Mac and the other hostages lying flat on the beach, caught in the cross fire along with a dozen or so gunmen.

The gunfire being laid down by Thorpe and the Danish officer was the only thing saving Harm and the Russian from being killed outright. Their two colleagues on the hill had managed to pin down more than a dozen men on the beach and were keeping at least two dozen more trapped inside the replenishment building.

But Harm also knew that this situation could not last forever. With the rate of fire coming from the ridge, Thorpe and the Dane would be running out of ammo very soon.

There really wasn't any time to think about it. Harm knew he had to act now. So he jammed the last clip into his M-16 and just started running. He was firing from his hip, like an action star in his own movie—the bullets even seemed to be leaving his gun in slow motion.

He was slipping and sliding on the rocky, slick beach, the ton of outerwear covering his body hindering him not in the least. The night air was absolutely thick with bullets, but even as Harm made his suicidal dash toward Mac and the hostages, he had to wonder why none of these bullets were hitting him.

But it was just a fleeting thought.

He was suddenly running right past the replenishment building and to his horror he saw the place was simply crawling with dark-suited gunmen who were, at that moment, positioning heavy weapons—cannons and machine guns—to shoot at the hostages, Thorpe, and the Dane up on the ridge. Gunfire was one thing; heavy weaponry was another. Once the men in the replenishment building got these big weapons in place, this little battle would be over quite quickly.

Harm kept on running, firing his weapon, though he was not sure if he was really hitting anything. It was just after he passed the replenishment building that he realized that Crekov was right on his heels. He was firing his rifle just as wildly as Harm was firing his.

Finally the pair of them reached the place where the gunmen were holding the hostages. The Russian skidded to a halt, lowered his weapon, and eliminated the startled gunmen with one long burst.

A second later, Harm fell in a heap right on top of Mac. He felt her fingers dig into him, right through his heavy parka. She immediately surrounded him in a bear hug.

"Holding down the fort here, Major?" he managed to kid her.

But Mac was not in a kidding mood.

"Just get us out of here," she said.

It was a good idea, of course. But exactly how was he going to it?

Harm looked around—their position was extremely tenuous. They had the hostages back, but there were still many armed men about. Some were shooting at them from the replenishment building, others from a work boat that had been tending the U-boat salvagers. The armed fishing boat itself was now but a few hundred yards away. Harm could see its decks were bristling with weapons and men to shoot them.

Even worse, from what he could tell, all firing from the top of the ridge had ceased. This could only mean one of two things: either Thorpe and the Dane had finally run out of ammo, or the six gunmen who had started the long climb up to silence those on the ridge had reached their destination and had coldly fulfilled their mission.

It was no surprise then that, at the moment, Harm felt like Custer at Little Big Horn.

But Custer hadn't had a guy named Mook with him.

"We must stay in place, here," Mook said, crawling through a hail of bullets, to where Harm, Mac, and the Russian were huddled. "I have a vision that we will be safe, if we just stay put."

"Stay put?" Harm asked him sternly. At the moment, that seemed like the last thing they should do. The gunmen in the replenishment building could be seen lowering a very large gun barrel in their direction. Heavy machine fire was now coming in from both the work boat and the armed fishing trawler. And Harm knew it was just a matter of time before some of the gunmen swung in behind them.

Then they'd be surrounded.

And then, they'd be done for.

Harm thought their only chance of survival—and it

was a slim one—was to try to make it to the northern slope of the bay, somehow climb it, and get to the other side. But it was at least one hundred yards to the bottom of this hill and about a fifty-foot climb, straight up, to its summit. They would be like ducks in a shooting gallery.

Still, it seemed better than the more grisly alternative.

"We *can't* stay here," Harm was saying to Mook.

"No, wait . . . listen to him," Mac said.

Harm looked over at her; she was still clutching his parka tightly with her fingers. "You're the one who just told me to get us out of here."

"I know," she said, "but sometimes it's wise to listen to him. He's plugged into something up here that we are not."

Harm looked over at the replenishment building and saw that the gunmen inside were about to fire the large cannon at them. He was sure its shells would be powerful enough to blow away the shallow rocks they were hiding behind. And then, it would blow them away as well.

"We just stay," Mook repeated again.

Harm was close to wit's end.

"For how long?" he yelled back at the shaman over the never-ending scream of bullets.

Mook closed his eyes and took a sniff of the air and finally replied, "Not long . . ."

Then he turned toward the sea, pointed, and said, "The friendly spirits are on their way."

Harm was in the middle of rolling his eyes when he felt Mac's fingers dig even deeper into his arm.

"Oh, my goodness," was just about all she could say when suddenly all noise of gunfire was drowned out by a tremendously loud screech.

Harm looked over his shoulder out toward the ocean

and saw three red lights coming right at him. They were very low, probably not much more than two hundred feet above the water, and they were moving tremendously fast.

The next thing he knew, he saw a long, white tube come speeding across the surface of the water itself. It went over the armed fishing trawler, over the submarine, and slammed into the replenishment building. There was a microsecond of a delay and then a tremendous explosion shook the beach and everything on it. Harm covered up Mac and Mook covered up Harm. The ground began shaking tremendously and a small avalanche of rocks, ice, and chunks of concrete began pelting them.

Finally, after ten long seconds, the earth stopped moving. But the air was still alive with the high-pitched screech. Harm dared to look up from the pile of arms and legs and saw what might have been the most beautiful flying thing in the world.

It was a B-1 bomber, streaking right over their heads.

Now there was cheering in his ears. Mac was screaming, Mook was laughing. Even the Russian was growling with delight. The replenishment building was no more. One precision-guided, two-thousand-pound bomb from the belly of the B-1 had simply vaporized the place—and everyone inside it.

But this did not mean they were all out of danger yet—as a sudden barrage of bullets going right over their heads so rightly emphasized.

There were still many gunmen out in the water, in the work boat and on the fishing trawler. They were now all firing at once toward the hostages' position.

But that's when they all heard yet another sound. This one, while mechanical, was certainly more quiet that the ear-splitting screech that had rocked the bay a few moments ago. Mook was pounding Harm on the shoulder and telling him to look up. Harm did, to find that a Dolphin helicopter was hovering right above them. Bud was hanging way out of the cabin, motioning frantically with his hands.

Harm didn't even stop to think about it. He began picking up the hostages and lifting them into Bud's outstretched arms. Harm felt adrenaline surge through his body as he picked up the burly Ininitka kayakers like they were bags of feathers and boosted them up to the tiny hovering helicopter with no problem at all.

The five kayakers somehow managed to squeeze into the cabin of the tiny helo—but now a problem developed. There was no more room inside the Dolphin, yet there were still six people on the ground: Harm, Mac, Mook, the Russian, and the two surviving Ininitka fishing-boat crewmen.

Harm thought the pilot might move away, safely drop off the kayakers, and then return for them. But it was clear that there was no time for anything like that. There was a work boat full of gunmen racing toward the shore. They were still firing their weapons. They would be on them long before the coast guard helo could ever make the round trip.

So its pilot simply brought his tiny aircraft down even closer to the ground. The Dolphin had two skids for its landing gear. The message from the pilot was clear: grab hold of the skids and hang on.

Now Harm was boosting people up again. The two fishing-boat crewmen grabbed on first and actually managed to climb up high enough to lock knees on the top of skids. Then up went Mook. He moved very quickly for an old guy, and proved strong enough to get a good grip for himself. Harm then lifted Mac up to the Ininitka men and the three of them pulled her up to the skid.

Then came a particularly brutal barrage of gunfire.

Harm and the Russian had to hit the deck. The Dolphin climbed a bit—it was getting unstable with the extra weight and its engine began smoking mightily. It came down for one more attempt—Harm knew it would be its last.

He turned to the Russian and locked his fingers together.

"You go first," he told the man, indicating he would boost him up.

But the Russian was shaking his head. "No, I boost you," he said. "If I stay behind, its okay. . . ."

More bullets went zinging by them.

"There's no way I'm leaving you behind, comrade!" Harm yelled back at him, knowing this was definitely not the place for such a discussion. "We don't both have to be heroes."

But it was funny what happened next. The Dolphin came down very close to the ground and suddenly both Harm and the Russian felt themselves being lifted up by many unseen hands. All of those on the skids—Mac included—had reached down as one and grabbed them. Now hanging on with all of their combined strength, the Dolphin finally started to move away.

The air was still being punctuated with tracer bullets. But then the mighty scream came back. Suddenly there was a bright white flash right above their heads and the B-1 swooped in again. A weapon came out of its bomb bay, skimmed the water briefly, and then slammed into the U-boat, destroying it utterly.

But the Dolphin began gyrating wildly as it got caught up in the exhaust wake left behind by the huge bomber, which was now streaking away to the east. Somehow the helo pilot was able to level off his aircraft and climb, slowly but surely, up to Lookout Point.

He topped the ridge just before both Harm and the

Russian's arms gave out. They both fell about thirty feet to the ground, luckily landing in a relatively soft snowbank. By the time they dug themselves out, the Dolphin was hovering above the field, letting all of the others off in a more conventional manner.

This done, the helo finally set down itself.

Mac ran into Harm's arms and hugged him for what seemed like a long time. Bud appeared and began shaking Harm's hand. Mook and his men were doing the Ininitka version of a group hug. The Russian, surprisingly enough, was on his knees, head bowed, giving some solitary thanks.

But then, a weird silence descended on the snow field. Harm turned to Crekov.

"What happened to Thorpe and the Dane?" he asked the Russian.

They began looking around, and it was Bud who saw the two unmoving figures at the top of the ridge. They all scrambled up to them, Harm fully expecting to see both men shot to pieces. But he had a pleasant surprise coming. Both men, while wounded, were still alive. Three bodies lying nearby told of a gun battle that Thorpe and Orbe had somehow won.

But this left them with yet another mystery. Six gunmen had been spotted climbing the ridge—and three had been shot dead by Thorpe and the Dane.

What had happened to the other three?

It took a few minutes of searching, but then it was Bud who came upon the grisly answer.

Down a path that came up the southern face of the ridge he discovered the bodies of the three other gunmen. They had been horribly mutilated.

"Polar bears?" Harm asked as the small band studied the gruesome scene.

"Evil spirits," Mook corrected him. "When they are

177

roused, they do not discriminate on who suffers their wrath.''

Harm took one last look at the three bodies. Whatever the reason, it was a bad way to go.

Their attention was now distracted by the sound of three consecutive explosions coming from the direction of the ocean. They all scrambled back to the top of the ridge—and saw a developing battle taking shape out at sea.

The armed fishing trawler was trying to make a get-away—and the *Sea Shadow II* was in close pursuit. They all saw two thin red beams suddenly flash out from the bow of the stealth ship and land on the bow of the re-treating trawler. They illuminated the ship for about five seconds, then there was one last explosion, and the armed fishing trawler was gone. All that was left in its wake was a puff of smoke and a thin layer of debris on top of the ocean.

Its work done, the stealth ship quickly moved back into the darkness.

"I don't think we were supposed to see that," Harm said.

"At least we know that the navy stuck to its word," Thorpe said. "They handled anything moving on the water and the air force took care of things on the land."

Harm just smiled wearily.

"Well, the next time they play each other in football, I'll take air force," Thorpe said. "They sure were there when we needed them."

Harm gave him a mock salute.

"You got yourself a bet," Harm replied.

twenty-two ✈

"I DON'T KNOW HOW YOU MANAGED TO TALK
me into this, Lieutenant."

Bud Roberts just smiled.

"I think it was right after you thanked me for saving
your life, sir," he replied. "You said: 'If there was anything I can do for you, just ask.' So I did."

Harm just smiled and continued trudging through the
deep snow.

"Next time I'll be sure to qualify such an offer," he
said.

They were walking toward a flat piece of icy range
about a half-mile west of Immaluost Station.

Things at the research facility had calmed down sub-
stantially in the last forty-eight hours. The three Russian
warships had departed that morning, after a huge well-
lubricated celebration the night before. Crekov the Russian had given Harm his E-mail address back in Russia.
Though Harm hardly knew the man, he felt like they
were brothers now after what they'd gone through. He
promised to stay in touch.

179

The Danes, too, had weighed anchor that morning. Harm thanked both the ship's captain and especially Lieutenant Orbe for their actions in the battle up at Lookout Point. The Danish captain graciously accepted Harm's thanks—and then handed him a bill for the Westland Lynx helicopter destroyed during the clash. Harm saw the forty-two million-dollar price tag, swallowed hard, and then promised to pass it on to his superiors in Washington.

Postbattle investigation up at Lookout Point confirmed what Harm and the others had theorized earlier: a band of Ukrainian mercenaries—possibly with the blessing of their government, possibly not—had come up to salvage the sunken U-boat in order to obtain a cache of clean steel for sale on the world's illegal arms market.

Sergei Bodachenko and Lieutenant Lapkin, going up to Lookout Point to be alone, happened upon the beginnings of the operation, and therefore had to be eliminated. In a strange way, however, their deaths had served a higher purpose. Had they not seen what they had, and paid with their lives for it, then the world would have been a slightly more dangerous place, with such a large amount of warhead-friendly clean steel circulating for sale to the highest bidder.

And Harm owed his life to Bud's quick thinking. Once Bud had put together the clues about clean steel and the possible Ukrainian involvement, Bud had convinced McKinney to call Thule and tell the special operations joint command there what they had learned. This had resulted in the arrival of the B-1 bomber and the *Sea Shadow II* in such a timely manner.

Then, going one further, Bud had prevailed upon McKinney to give him the use of the Dolphin and its pilot in order to fly up to Lookout Point. Had he not done this, the tragedy on the beach might have been far worse than it was.

So Harm definitely owed one to Bud. But how did he know the stocky lieutenant would come up with such an unorthodox way for him to pay him back?

They reached the flattened ice plain and finally stopped for a breath. It was a very sunny day, and the temperature was a balmy twenty below. Bud was carrying a thermometer with him; Harm was carrying a duffel bag.

Bud reached a particular spot he'd previously staked out from the air and checked the thermometer.

"Okay, sir," he said. "I think we are all set."

Harm opened up the duffel bag.

"Okay, let's just get this over with," he said in mock irritation.

Bud just shrugged.

"Aye, sir," he replied, adding, "I'll try the two wood please."

Harm just shook his head, reached inside the duffel bag, and came up with the correct golf club. It was part of a set Thorpe just happened to have on hand. Meanwhile, Bud was carefully unwrapping three orange golf balls which he had encased in ice almost two days ago.

He placed the first golf ball on a tee and took a few practice swings, looking rather comical doing so in his heavy outerwear.

"If my theory is right, sir," Bud said, "this shot should go a mile."

Harm just rolled his eyes. Bud reared back and came down with a swoop on the golf ball. It exploded off the tee—and went screaming up into the calm, frigid air.

Harm let out a long whistle—the ball *did* seem to travel a very long way.

"You know, you might have something here, Lieutenant," he said, authentically surprised. "Give it another try."

Bud teed up his second ball, took a couple more practice swings, then gave it a whack. Again the ball took off like it was heading into orbit.

"Amazing," Harm said. "Do it again."

But Bud was suddenly stuttering. "I . . . I really . . . d-d-don't know if . . . I should do that," he managed to croak out.

Harm gave him a look and saw that Bud was staring at a point just off to their left. Harm turned to see three polar bears moving very quickly in their direction.

"Oh my God!" Harm yelled.

They started running, down off the icy plain, and into the deep snow beyond. The bears gave chase.

"We're never going to make it!" he yelled over to Bud. But now the lieutenant was smiling again. He was looking straight up. Harm did, too—and saw that there was a helicopter hovering high above them.

It was the Dolphin helo, its ultraquiet engine masking any announcement of its approach.

Whoever was inside the helo saw their predicament, and the helo started coming down very fast.

It landed nearby, and Harm and Bud scrambled aboard, leaving the golf implements behind.

Only after he was safely inside did Harm realize that it was Mac riding in the copilot's seat. She turned and gave them both a very stern look.

"I can't let you two out of my sight for five minutes," she said. "Luckily we were passing by this way or we would have needed toothpicks to recover your bodies. You should be thankful."

Harm and Bud just looked at each other and clasped hands. She was right, of course—the Ininitka spirits must have been looking down on them again.

"And where, may I ask, are you going?" Harm whispered in Mac's ear.

"Well," she replied, "now that I'm forced to take you along for the ride, you'll just have to wait and see for yourself."

They flew on for another ten minutes, finally setting down at the Ininitka settlement. But this was not their destination. They were simply picking up another passenger.

Mook came out to meet the helo, and with a great cheer from just about everyone in the village, he climbed aboard the helo, carrying a bag containing a fishing net on his back.

He looked at Bud and Harm and smiled. "So the heroes want to see a bit of magic, too, do they?"

Mook then gave the Dolphin pilot a small map and they took off again. They flew for another fifteen minutes before setting down on a small beach, approximately thirty miles north of the Ininitka settlement.

They piled out, Harm and Bud still in the dark as to why they had come to this particular spot.

Mook unraveled the fishing net, closed its ends off, and then gave them all a smile.

"I promised this fair lady that if she helped us with our ghost problems, I would show her this very magical place," he announced.

Mac bowed to him slightly. "I am the one who is honored," she said.

Harm just rolled his eyes. "Is this why you wanted to stay up here an extra day?" he asked her. "To see some voodoo?"

"Did you really want to stay just to be Bud's caddy?" she shot back.

Harm was stung, but only a little.

"But now you're going to make this old guy embarrass himself," he told her in a whisper.

"Why do you say that?" she wanted to know.

"Magic? Evil spirits? That story you told me about these guys claiming they're responsible for the Loch Ness monster?" He laughed. "I mean, come on. . . ."

Mook had finished laying out the net and had heard a piece of their conversation.

He smiled again.

"This is even better when there are nonbelievers about," he said.

Then he motioned for Bud to help him and together they marched into the shallow water of the beach and laid the net down.

Then Mook let out a great whoop—and suddenly the water around the net began moving.

Harm felt his eyes go wide—he thought for sure he'd finally gone around the bend. Hundreds of fish were leaping out of the water—and going right into the net!

He'd never seen anything like it.

"Wow," was all he could say at the moment.

Mac was smiling from ear to ear; Bud and the chopper pilot were simply amazed.

"You see, there *are* some things you don't know about, Commander," Mac razzed him as the nonstop stream of fish continued hurling themselves into the net.

Harm just shook his head. He was legitimately baffled.

"I guess you're right," he said. "But I'll tell you something—just when I think things up here can't get any crazier . . ."

That's when he felt Mac's fingers digging into his arm again.

"Don't you *dare* . . . ," she said.